I0593343

DESOLATION

PETER MULRANEY

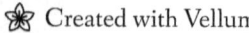

Dedicated to the Friends of the Burra Railway Station

CHAPTER 1

ON A WARM SUNDAY morning in mid-November, 1991, Sue Edwards pulled into the driveway of the house in Essex Street, Burra, that she shared with her seventeen-year-old daughter, Jane. Sue was feeling good. She'd spent the night in Clare with Kevin Marshall, the new man in her life. The first night she'd spent with a man since her husband had died when Jane was a five-year old.

She wondered what Jane and her boyfriend, eighteen-year-old Andrew White, thought about her finally giving in to Kevin and shook her head. What did it matter? The kids these days didn't wait for anything or anyone's approval. Jane and Andrew had been at it since the start of the school year, ever since they'd decided they were a couple going places. They'd told her about their big plans that didn't include spending the rest of their lives in Burra.

Sue knew she was going to miss them once they went off to university in Adelaide at the end of summer, but she had her own life to live. Maybe Kevin's recent arrival in her life had been more than just good timing. Perhaps it was the universe's way of looking after her. She liked being looked after.

It had been a struggle bringing up Jane on her own, even with the life insurance money. At least she'd been able to pay off the mortgage and buy a new car. Not things she'd have been able to do otherwise on her wages.

Sue looked at the house. Built of local stone, it had stood for eighty years and would no doubt be still standing long after she'd gone. The garden looked like it could use a drink and there were a few dry weeds visible over the edge of the gutter at the front of the house. Something she'd need to attend to soon or at least ask Kevin to do something about.

The curtains were still drawn in Jane's room. Sue looked at her watch. It was ten past eleven. Jane was an early riser, even when Andrew stayed over, and neither of them drank much. She wondered if they'd decided to spend the night at Andrew's house after all.

Sue slipped out of the car, retrieved her overnight bag from the back seat, and made her way around to the back door. It was locked. She inserted her key into the lock, opened the door, and stepped into the mudroom at the rear of the house. Andrew's overnight bag was still on the table by the door where he'd placed it when he'd arrived the previous evening.

A tingle of concern wriggled along Sue's spine. She opened the door into the corridor that bisected the length of the house. Sunlight streamed through the stained glass panes of the front door onto the hardwood floorboards of the passageway. The only sound was the thud of her overnight bag landing on the floor.

The door to Jane's room was open. Sue stopped in the doorway, half expecting to see them entangled in the bedclothes. The bed was empty. It looked like it hadn't been slept in. There were no clothes strewn about the room. Jane's keys were not on her bedside table.

'Jane!'

No answer. She walked back along the corridor to the kitchen to see whether Jane had left her a note stuck on the fridge under her angel magnet. They had one each and never left the house without leaving a message about where they were going on the fridge door. Sue's blue angel was there, holding the piece of paper with the contact details of the motel where she and Kevin had spent the night. Next to it, Jane's green angel still held the invitation to the end of school year party at Sally Nelson's.

Obviously they hadn't come back to the house after the party. Sue went into the hallway, lifted the telephone out of its cradle on the wall and punched in the White's number.

'Hi, Cynthia. Are the kids there?'

'Aren't they at your place?'

'I just got in from Clare. There's nobody here, and Jane's bed hasn't been slept in. Thought they must have decided to sleep at your place.'

'Well, they're not here. Maybe they're still at the Nelsons',' said Cynthia. 'Perhaps it turned into a sleepover.'

Sue felt the weight lift from her chest. 'Didn't think of that.'

'How was Clare?' says Cynthia.

'Tell you all about it tonight,' said Sue, picturing Cynthia leaning on the bench in the hospital kitchen as they prepared that evening's meals for the aged care residents who made up the bulk of the hospital's patients.

Sue ended the call, retrieved the party invitation from

under Jane's fridge magnet, and punched in the digits Sally Nelson had printed on it.

'Oh, hello, Mrs Edwards.'

'Sally, is Jane there?'

'What?'

'She's not here and she's not at Andrew's. I was wondering if they slept over at your place.'

'They left here around midnight.'

―――――

Sue was at a loss. Where could they be? It wasn't like they'd get lost on the way home. It was only a ten minute walk from the Nelsons' in Welsh Place around to her house in Essex Street, and none of it along the highway that snaked its way through Burra. They didn't even have to cross Burra Creek or walk through the main part of town.

She called Kevin.

'I don't know what to do, Kev. There's no sign of the kids and no-one seems to know where they are.'

'Who have you called?' said Kevin.

'She hasn't been home,' said Sue, not hearing his question.

'I'll be right over.'

While she waited for Kevin to arrive, Sue called the Owens' number. Rebecca and Jane had been best friends ever since they'd started school.

'Becky, do you know where Jane is?'

'Haven't heard from her since last night. Is something wrong?'

'I don't know where she is.'

'She said they were going to your place when we were

leaving the party,' said Rebecca. 'Dad offered them a lift but they said they'd walk.'

'Who else was at the party?' said Sue.

'Only Lydia, but her Mum picked her up around eleven. They were going down to Adelaide today.'

'Can you call me if you hear anything?'

'Sure, Mrs Edwards.'

Sue pictured the group, the four girls and Andrew, who called themselves 'The Book Club'. They were the academically inclined members of their year twelve class with aspirations of going to university and escaping the small town confines of Burra. The group had become close, especially over the last couple of years in which they had attracted some unwanted attention from some of their less academically inclined classmates.

Andrew especially had had a rough time of it in a schoolyard where sporting prowess and animal magnetism were held in higher regard than academic success. It hadn't helped that he was the son of a townie and had four girlfriends, one of whom was the most popular senior girl at Burra Community School.

Sue hoped they hadn't become the unwitting victims of one last school year prank.

Kevin listened to Sue's concerns. He'd only met Andrew and Jane a couple of weeks ago and they'd struck him as sensible kids.

'This is so unlike her,' said Sue. 'She knows I worry if I don't know where she is.'

'There will be an explanation,' said Kevin. 'There always is.'

They heard car doors slam and the crunch of boots on the gravel driveway.

'Maybe that's them,' said Kevin.

But it wasn't. Michael and Cynthia White came in through the back door.

'Anything?' said Michael. 'Cynthia's beside herself.'

'I don't know what to think,' said Cynthia. 'He's never done anything like this before.'

They stood looking at each other across Sue's kitchen table.

'I think we should talk to the police,' said Kevin. 'They'll know what to do.'

'Are you sure?' said Michael.

'They'll at least know how to arrange a search,' said Kevin.

CHAPTER 2

Sergeant Ross Sloane was enjoying a barbecue lunch under the pergola at the rear of the house that came with his position. He heard the telephone ring inside the house. A few moments later, his younger daughter appeared in the back doorway.

'Dad!'

She had his attention.

'There's a man on the phone for you.'

Ross put down his beer, excused himself, and went into the house. Interruptions to his day off were all part of his role as the officer in charge of the Burra Police Station. He may not have been on duty today but he was always on standby.

The call was from the Operations Centre in Adelaide, which handled calls to the police assistance line when there was no-one manning the local station. He wrote down the details and hung up, wondering if he had a problem or some overly anxious parents. Whichever it was, he knew he'd better meet with them and go over the details.

He went back into the yard where his wife was sitting at

the table with their guests, one of his wife's colleagues and her husband.

'Sorry, folks, got to go out for a while. Shouldn't be too long. Need to speak to some concerned parents about a couple of teenagers that didn't come home last night.'

'Who are the kids?' said Mary, who taught at the Community School.

'Jane Edwards and Andrew White,' said Ross.

'Can't see them being trouble,' said Mary. 'They're a couple of the brightest kids I've ever taught.'

'Apparently they went to a party last night and nobody has seen them since.'

'Hope none of the boys have pulled one last prank for the end of the school year,' said Mary's colleague, the deputy principal of the school. 'I had to haul a few of them over the coals for harassing Andrew earlier in the year.'

'Any names come to mind?'

She screwed up her face and stroked her chin. 'You might want to start with John Grant if you have to start asking questions.'

'I'll keep that in mind,' said Ross, adding Grant's name to his note.

Ross drove to the address in Essex Street and parked behind the white Toyota Hilux with Burra Plumbing signage across its tailgate in front of the house. He wondered what the connection was between Kevin Marshall and Sue Edwards.

He recognised Michael White's silver Mitsubishi parked in the driveway behind Sue's blue Corolla. Recognising people's cars was something that came with the territory when you were a policeman in a place like Burra. He walked across the front yard, mounted the two steps leading onto the veranda and knocked on the front door.

Kevin Marshall opened the door and grinned as he recognised the local police sergeant standing on the veranda in his civvies. 'G'day, Ross. Sorry to bugger up your Sunday.'

'Wasn't expecting to see you here, Kev,' said Ross. 'Does Sue have a plumbing problem as well?'

'We're friends,' said Kevin, blushing slightly. 'You'd better come in. She's beside herself.'

Ross followed Kevin through the house to the kitchen, where the others were sitting around the table. There was no need for introductions.

'We've rung all their friends,' said Michael. 'No-one's seen them since they left the Nelsons' last night.'

'What were they doing there?' said Ross.

'End of school year party,' said Sue, pointing to the invitation on the front of the fridge.

Ross looked at the invitation and noted the details. 'Who else was at this party?'

'It was only the book club,' said Sue.

'The book club?' said Ross.

'Jane, Andrew, Sally Nelson, Becky Owens and Lydia Parks,' said Cynthia. 'They've been friends for years.'

Ross wondered what sort of lad hung around with a group of girls. It certainly wasn't something he had done at school. He recalled what his wife's friend had said about Andrew being harassed by some of the other boys and wondered if he was gay.

'We haven't been able to contact the Parks,' said Michael. 'Apparently they're spending the day in Adelaide.'

'Any chance Jane and Andrew went with them?' said Ross.

'She would have left a note,' said Sue.

'And, Andrew would have told us,' said Cynthia.

'Either of them in any trouble?' said Ross.

'Not recently,' said Michael. 'Andrew copped a bit of flak from some of the other boys at school earlier in the year, but that all died down after the school took action.'

'What about Jane?'

'Voted most popular girl in her class,' said Sue.

'That get her any undue attention?' said Ross.

'I don't think so,' said Sue. 'Everyone knew she and Andrew were an item.'

'Which is why that Grant boy gave him a hard time,' said Cynthia. 'Apparently he was upset Jane wasn't interested in him.'

So much for him being gay, thought Ross, as he leant against the doorframe. 'I know you're worried. I would be worried too if it was one of my kids, but it's early days for a missing persons case. Most teenagers that go missing turn up again within a few days, but it won't hurt for me to put out an alert in case they've left the area.'

'Okay,' said Sue. 'Do you need some photos or anything?'

'A recent photo would help,' said Ross, 'along with a description of what they were wearing.'

'That bit's the easy part,' said Sue. 'The book club uniform. Jeans, white shirt, sneakers, and a navy blue sweatshirt.'

Ross wrote that in his notebook. 'And, is anything missing from their rooms?'

'What do you mean?' said Michael.

'Things they'd take if they were planning a trip,' said Ross.

'Andrew's overnight bag is still where he left it in the mudroom when he got here yesterday,' said Sue, 'and I can't see anything missing from Jane's room, apart from her house keys and the clothes she was wearing.'

It was starting to sound to Ross like these kids had either made an impromptu decision or something more sinister had happened to them.

'I'll get an alert out and start asking around,' said Ross. 'I'll get my officers to door knock the routes they could have taken last night to see if anybody heard anything or saw them. What time did they leave this party?'

'Around midnight according to Sally,' said Sue.

Ross didn't like their chances of someone seeing them at that hour. 'And, where were you last night, Sue?'

'We spent the night in Clare,' said Kevin.

'And we were home with the telly,' said Cynthia.

'Andrew was staying over with Jane,' said Sue, 'seeing I was going to be in Clare.'

'That unusual?' said Ross.

'Not really,' said Sue. 'Andrew stays over most Saturday nights.'

Something else that had changed since he had been a teenager living at home, thought Ross. There had been no way Mary's parents would have allowed that to happen under their roof.

The Whites smiled, as if they'd been reading his thoughts.

'Let me know when you've spoken to the Parks,' said Ross. 'Call me at home. There won't be anybody at the station until tomorrow morning.'

Sergeant Sloane issued a media alert through Adelaide when he got home in case they were dealing with runaways. After all, Jane was still a minor, even if she had gone willingly. Then he changed into his uniform and drove around town, asking if anyone had seen Jane or Andrew.

By late afternoon, he was worried enough to express his concern to his superior at Regional Headquarters and to call in his three constables, who he sent out to door knock the streets between the Nelsons' house in Welsh Place and Sue Edwards' home in Essex Street. They came back empty handed.

First thing Monday morning, Michael White called to let him know Jane and Andrew had not turned up and were not with the Parks. Sergeant Sloane updated his superior.

At midday, a team of detectives arrived from Regional Headquarters in Port Pirie. They took over the briefing room in the police station and set about interviewing everyone who knew Jane and Andrew, including the boys who had harassed them during the school year.

While the detectives conducted their interviews, Ross Sloane had his constables take a good look around. Although Burra was now the service centre of a farming community, it was a tourist destination because it had started life as a mining town. That meant there were plenty of places to dump a body if you were that way inclined, including the lake that filled the open cut pit of the Monster Mine.

In early December, the disappearance of Jane Edwards and Andrew White was declared a major crime and received significant media coverage. However, efforts to locate them proved fruitless, despite the government offering a fifty thousand dollar reward.

Over time, the case slowly faded from public consciousness to become another unsolved mystery, one which was resurrected every few years whenever the media needed something sensational to talk about.

CHAPTER 3

ON THE LAST Wednesday morning of November, 2021, Sergeant Bob Davenport sat at his desk in the Burra Police Station scrolling through emails and half listening to Radio National. Someone from the Bureau of Meteorology was describing the weather pattern, which had delivered five times their average monthly rainfall in a matter of a few days earlier in the month, as an atmospheric stream of moisture driven by warmer than usual waters off the north coast of Australia.

Climate change, thought Bob, leaning back in his chair to listen. Everybody he'd spoken to in town was talking climate change. He hadn't seen that much water flowing in any of the local creeks ever, and neither had any of the old-timers who had spent their entire lives in Burra.

When he'd been posted to Burra, in what the locals referred to as the mid-north of South Australia, Bob had never imagined he'd be setting up road blocks because there was water on the road. Dust storms and the occasional grass fire, not floods, was what he'd expected to deal with.

His train of thought was interrupted by a ripple of sound from the telephone on his desk.

'Burra Police Station.'

'That you, Bob? Chris Marshall.'

Chris Marshall was the National Parks and Wildlife Service ranger that looked after the Red Banks Conservation Park, located fifteen kilometres east of Burra, out where there was usually more red dirt and rocks than grass, although the conservation park was partially covered with mallee woodland. The only times Bob had been to the park was to attend the picnic races to oversee crowd control, but that was in the days before Covid. It wasn't a place that attracted much police attention otherwise.

'What can I do for you, Chris?'

'I've found a skeleton,' said Chris. 'Think you'd better come and take a look. It doesn't look all that ancient to me.'

Bob didn't know much about skeletons, ancient or modern, but he knew where he could find someone who did if he'd need an expert opinion.

'Where will I find you?'

'Meet me in the camping ground and, Bob, come in one of your four-wheel drives. Tracks in the park are still a bit soft.'

Bob slowed the Hilux and turned off Goyder Highway after the sign for Red Banks at Eastern Road and made his way along the unsealed road towards the park. At the entrance to the park he stopped and engaged the four-wheel drive, before driving through the open gate and following the track to the camping ground. As he entered the camp site, Chris

Marshall climbed out of his vehicle, another white Toyota Hilux spattered with red mud.

'What are you doing out here?' said Bob, shaking hands with Chris, despite the Covid protocols he was meant to be following.

'Checking the place over before we reopen. Haven't had this much rain in these parts since Adam was a boy.'

'Atmospheric rivers according to some bloke on the radio,' said Bob. 'Another way of saying climate change, if you ask me.'

'You're probably right,' said Chris. 'Anyway, whatever it was, it dumped enough water to wash out a couple of gullies leading down to the creek. That's where I spotted the skeleton.'

'What makes you think it's human?' said Bob. 'I thought this place was famous for giant wombats.'

'Have a look at this,' said Chris, taking out his smartphone and opening the photos app before passing it to Bob.

'See what you mean,' said Bob, gazing at the partially exposed human skull in the photograph. 'Want to show me where you took that?'

Chris led Bob along a trail between the trees and down towards Baldina Creek, whose tall banks of red earth gave the park its name. Five minutes later, Chris stepped off the trail and Bob followed him for about twenty metres to the edge of a gully showing recent signs of water erosion.

'There,' said Chris, pointing to a white human skull, staring at them with blank eye sockets from a patch of wet red soil at the bottom of the gully, roughly two metres down from where they stood.

Bob took a couple of photos with his own smartphone

and tied a piece of crime scene tape to a tree to mark the point where they'd veered off the walking trail.

'I'll need to get someone from Adelaide to work out how long it's been there,' said Bob, 'which means I'll need to treat the park as a crime scene until we sort that out.'

'That shouldn't be a problem,' said Chris. 'I'll lock the gate. It's still too wet for campers and day trippers in any case.'

They walked back towards their vehicles in the camping ground. 'Any human bones ever been found here before?' said Bob, thinking the park could contain an unmarked indigenous burial ground since most were only discovered by accident, thanks to Australia's colonial past.

'Not to my knowledge,' said Chris, 'but that skull doesn't look all that old to me, which is why I called you.'

'I'm no expert on bones,' said Bob. 'We'll know soon enough if they're old or not.'

They walked in silence. Bob hoped the skeleton belonged in the distant past. He didn't fancy having to open an investigation to work out how a skeleton ended up being buried in the conservation park.

'You know, when I was a kid,' said Chris, 'a couple of local teenagers disappeared one night. No-one's heard from them since.'

'How long ago was that?' said Bob, thinking there'd be some sort of record in the station's archives or down in Adelaide.

'Be thirty years this month,' said Chris. 'I was eleven when it happened.'

Bob stopped walking. Bits of an ancient news story played in his head. 'Before my time in the force but I think I remember that. Boy and a girl, wasn't it?'

'Jane Edwards and Andrew White,' said Chris.

'You knew them?' said Bob. Chris was a local.

'Not really,' said Chris, 'but Jane's mother is my step-mother. It's a long story.'

Shit, thought Bob, this could turn ugly. 'We'd better keep this to ourselves until we know what we're dealing with, Chris. I'd rather not upset your stepmother unless I have to.'

'Let's hope I'm wrong,' said Chris, 'and it turns out to be some indigenous bloke from a long time ago that only needs a proper reburial.'

Bob rostered his constables to secure the park, even though it was literally in the middle of nowhere. They only had to sit in their vehicles outside the gate, but there was no way he was giving anyone higher up the chain an opportunity to kick his arse for not securing a crime scene. He'd rather take the flak for wasting resources if it turned out the remains were something the SA Museum could take off his hands.

He reported the finding of a skull at Red Banks Conservation Park to his inspector at Regional Headquarters in Port Pirie, who told him to secure the scene and wait for the crime scene investigators to arrive from Adelaide.

'Sir, the ranger who came across the skull reminded me that a couple of teenagers went missing from here around thirty years ago.'

'You'd better sit on that information for the time being, Sergeant. We don't want to get anyone's hopes up,' said the inspector. 'Can you rely on your ranger mate to keep his mouth shut?'

'He's agreed to keep it quiet until we know how old the

skull is, sir,' said Bob, wondering if the inspector would notice he'd already taken steps to keep a lid on the situation.

'Good thinking, Sergeant. Keep me in the loop once CSI arrive.' Then the inspector was gone.

Bob queried the cold case database and discovered the files from the investigation into the disappearance of Jane Edwards and Andrew White were in storage in Adelaide.

He made a note of the case ID. There was no need to get excited. He knew if it turned out to be either of them he might get to break the news to the parents but he wouldn't be getting the case. That would fall to some poor detective who'd be tasked with the almost impossible feat of solving a thirty-year-old puzzle.

Bob turned his attention back to the present day. With his constables taking it in turns to keep an eye on the conservation park, anything needing immediate police attention would fall to him. Fortunately, Burra was a quiet law-abiding town most days of the week.

A few minutes after four that afternoon, Bob Davenport escorted Dr Stephen Lewis, the forensic anthropologist from Adelaide University who had arrived with the crime scene investigators, to the gully where the skull lay partially exposed in the damp red soil.

Bob stood on the edge of the gully and watched as Dr Lewis made his way down to the bottom and examined the skull.

'First impression is you have a crime scene, Sergeant. This is not old enough to be of any interest to science.'

'You can tell that just by looking at it?' said Bob.

Dr Lewis smiled. 'Ever seen the collection of indigenous skeletons in the museum, Sergeant?'

'Can't say that I have,' said Bob, 'but I read something about them being prepared for reburial.'

'Yes, and not before time,' said Dr Lewis, 'but they're old. Hundreds if not thousands of years old. I've been lucky enough to study them. This is a very young skull. There's a difference.'

'What happens now?' said Bob.

'You've probably got a whole skeleton from what I can see, Sergeant. We'll excavate it as a crime scene and see if we can work out who it is you have here.'

CHAPTER 4

PAT TRAVERS OPENED his eyes and immediately closed them again. God it was bright. He turned his head and looked at the alarm clock. Shit! He must have gone back to sleep. If he wasn't out the door in twenty minutes he'd miss the bus.

Pat hated being late for work. He leapt out of bed and set a record for the four-minute shower but couldn't maintain his momentum, since he'd forgotten to iron a shirt before going to bed and there was no way he was going to work in a wrinkled shirt.

The bus was at the end of the street, turning onto the main road, a good hundred metres down from the bus stop in front of his house, when he finally made it to the front door. It would be another fifteen minutes before the next one arrived. He went back inside and wolfed down a pot of strawberry yoghurt for breakfast.

When he finally arrived at Angas Street, twenty minutes later than normal, he was called in to Detective Inspector Smith's office.

'I know you're an old-timer, Detective Sergeant, but the

shift starts at eight,' said Inspector Smith, with a smile. 'You got a new girlfriend or something?'

'Just getting old, I'm afraid,' said Pat. 'Slept through the bloody alarm. Wish I could promise it won't happen again, sir, but I don't think I can guarantee my own word on that.' He wasn't about to disclose he'd spent the night polishing off a bottle of shiraz on his own, before falling into bed after midnight. He wished he had a new girlfriend to blame, but he'd given up on that dream some time ago.

'Try not to make it too often, Pat.' The inspector picked up a blue lever arch folder from his desk and handed it to him. 'I want you to take a look at this and see if we can progress it.'

Pat glanced at the folder. The cover was faded. He assumed it was another cold case that had been pulled from the archives, since reviewing cold cases seemed to be all the inspector would let him do these days. 'Another cold case, sir?'

'It's been on the books for thirty years as a missing persons case. You may have heard of it. Edwards and White?'

That rang a bell. Pat queried his internal search engine. 'Isn't this one of Port Pirie's cases?' said Pat, wondering why he was being asked to look at it.

'There's been a development,' said Inspector Smith. 'It's no longer a missing persons case. Their remains were excavated last week from a shallow grave in a conservation park outside Burra. I'll send you the details.'

'What exactly do you want me to look for, sir?'

'I know it's a long shot, Pat, especially after thirty years, but see if you can find anything that might point us to their killer.'

'Can I have someone to help me with this, sir? Two heads are always better than one when sifting through these old cases.'

'I can give you DC Palumbo,' said Inspector Smith. 'She's not working on anything major at the moment.'

Great, thought Pat. Lina Palumbo was the new kid no-one wanted on their team, no matter what the game was. 'Thank you, sir.'

'She's got the making of a good detective, Pat. She's smart, but she needs someone like you to take her under his wing and show her how to be a good team player,' said Inspector Smith.

'Leave it to me, sir.'

Pat returned to his desk in the squad room, wondering what he'd done to be lumbered with DC Lina Palumbo. He hadn't worked on a case with her since she'd joined the squad, but he'd heard plenty of complaints from those who had. He wondered how long he'd be saddled with her. Then he looked at the folder the inspector had given him and wondered why he'd been assigned the case. Obviously, no-one up the chain of command thought it was worth devoting their top resources to solving the thirty-year mystery hidden within its pages.

It didn't take Pat long to confirm his suspicions as to why the inspector had asked him to review the case. They had precious little hard evidence. The forensic analysis had identified the skeletal remains from the victims' dental records. In addition to the skeletons, the grave had yielded two metal belt buckles, a Timex watch, a set of house keys, the metallic parts of two pairs of Levi Strauss jeans, all badly corroded, and four desiccated Adidas Rome sneakers.

The only piece of evidence pointing to their killer, which had survived thirty years of burial with the victims' bodies, was a spent .22LR cartridge. An artefact from one of the most common forms of ammunition in the world, let alone in Australia. But at least it would have the ballistics' equivalent of the fingerprint of the weapon that had struck the cartridge to discharge it.

Pat searched through the forensic report for cause of death. Jane Edwards had been shot in the head from close range but the crime scene investigators had not located the round. Andrew White had been killed by a blow to the back of his head with a blunt instrument. Time and decay had removed all evidence of any other trauma the victims had endured.

The victims had disappeared in 1991. Five years before the upheaval in Australian gun laws, following the Port Arthur massacre in Tasmania, had removed hundreds of thousands of weapons from circulation. Pat didn't like their chances of ever finding the weapon that had fired the round from the cartridge found with the skeletons. The killer could have surrendered the weapon during one of the amnesties and gun buybacks, and all surrendered weapons had been destroyed.

This investigation was definitely going to be a long shot.

Pat booked a room away from the noise of the telephones in the squad room and met with Lina Palumbo to discuss their case.

Lina was tall with long legs, and twenty years younger than Pat. She'd become a detective around six months ago, after eight years in Uniform. Pat was a thirty-year veteran of the force. He'd been at the academy when Jane Edwards and Andrew White had gone missing and met their fate. He'd been a detective for twenty of those years, and a detective sergeant for twelve. He didn't have any delusions about rising beyond his current rank. His life had flatlined after breast cancer had taken Pam from him five years ago, and he knew he was simply filling in time until he was ready to retire.

Lina smiled as she entered and sat opposite Pat at the table in the middle of the small room. He couldn't help but notice her perfume and hoped he wasn't emitting an unpleasant body odour.

'Sergeant,' said Lina.

'Call me Pat when we're together,' said Pat. 'Let's leave the formal stuff for formal occasions, okay?'

'Okay, Pat.'

She smiled, but Pat thought she looked a little uneasy about using his first name.

'What are we working on?'

'This.' Pat pushed the folder Inspector Smith had retrieved from the archives across the table to her.

Lina opened the folder and read the first page, which summarised its contents. 'Are we doing a cold case? I've never worked on one of these.'

'It's an old case, I'll grant you that, but we're about to upgrade it to a homicide investigation.'

'What? Just the two of us?'

Pat smiled. She wasn't as stupid as some of his colleagues

had claimed. 'Inspector Smith has asked me to do an initial review.'

'Why? Is there going to be an inquest after thirty years?'

'No, Lina. There's new evidence.'

'Oh, I should have twigged when you said we were upgrading the case to a homicide. I take it by new evidence you mean we have some bodies?'

'Skeletons, actually, but they've been identified through their dental records.'

Lina took out her notebook and pen. 'Do we know how they were killed?'

'That's in the forensic report.'

'Do we know when they were killed?'

Pat leant back in his chair. 'Given what's in that folder, I think it's safe to assume they were killed around the time they disappeared.'

'Has anyone informed the parents?'

'That's being taken care of by Port Pirie,' said Pat. 'Suspect they'll get someone local who knows them.'

'Do we have anything to go on?'

'Well, what we'll do is read everything we have on file, all the records of interview, and then we'll need to reinterview everyone who is still alive.'

Lina put down her pen. 'That sounds pretty boring, Pat.'

'A lot of what we do is boring, Lina. If you didn't want to do boring, why'd you become a detective?

'It's okay, Pat. I like looking for patterns and connections, and besides, I've heard you're safe to work with.'

'Safe?' said Pat.

Lina smiled. 'All the girls say you're a gentleman, Pat, not like some of the others who are more interested in our tits than our brains.'

Pat crossed his arms and leant forward to rest his elbows on the table between them. 'You've got tits, have you?'

Lina punched him gently in the arm.

Pat rubbed his arm in mock surprise. He was starting to like Lina Palumbo. She reminded him of his daughter. 'Shall we make a start?'

CHAPTER 5

SUE MARSHALL WAS MAKING herself a coffee in the kitchen at the rear of her house in Essex Street when she heard the front doorbell ring. She stopped what she was doing and wondered who she'd find when she opened the door. Her friends knew to come around to the back of the house, so she knew it wouldn't be one of them. She walked up the passageway and opened the door to a policeman standing on her veranda. He looked uncomfortable. She felt a sense of dread.

'Sue Marshall?'

'Yes.'

'My name's Bob Davenport. I'm the sergeant at the local police station.' He twisted his hat in his hands. 'Do you think I could come in? I've got some rather unpleasant news for you.'

Sue felt her knees knock together. 'Has something happened to Chris?'

'No. Chris is fine.'

There was concern in his eyes. It was obvious he was worried about how she was going to take his news.

'It's about Jane.'

Sue didn't know how to respond to that. She'd been waiting to learn her daughter's fate for thirty years but a lot of life had happened while she'd been waiting. She'd known right from the start Jane wouldn't be coming back and now, after all this time, here was a policeman saying he had news about her. 'You'd better come in then.'

She led him through to the kitchen. 'I was just making coffee. Do you want one?'

'White, no sugar, thanks.'

The policeman sat at the table while she reheated the water in the electric kettle and found a second mug for his coffee. 'What did you say your name was again?'

'Bob Davenport.'

Sue hadn't had much to do with the police since she'd retired from her job at the hospital. She couldn't recall seeing Bob around town.

'Have you been here long, Bob?'

'Around five years.'

Five years, thought Sue. That's a long time for someone to be in town without her knowing. More of a reflection on her lifestyle than his.

'Where were you before you came to Burra?'

'Port Pirie.'

Sue placed the cups of coffee on the table and sat down opposite him. He didn't look old enough to have been a policeman when Jane and Andrew had disappeared, but she thought he was probably old enough to have heard about it when they did. 'Where were you when they disappeared?'

'I was at school, doing year ten. I remember hearing about it on the news.' He smiled. 'Never imagined I'd be sitting here telling you what happened to Jane.'

Sue knew she couldn't keep stalling him forever with her questions. 'So, what have you come to tell me, Bob?'

'There's no easy way to say this, Mrs Marshall. Jane's dead, and it looks like she was killed around the time she and Andrew disappeared.'

Sue caught her breath and then remembered to breathe. It all seemed so matter of fact. Confirmation of what she'd already convinced herself of what had happened. She'd already drained the tank on her emotions, years ago.

'What about Andrew?'

'They're both dead, I'm afraid. We're treating their deaths as suspicious.'

They sat in silence.

Sue picked up her coffee and took a sip. 'I was right all along, then. I knew they hadn't run away.'

'I'm sorry,' said Bob.

'Where'd you find them?'

'Out at Red Banks,' said Bob. 'All that rain we had last month uncovered their grave in one of the gullies feeding water into the creek that runs through the park.'

'Red Banks? That's one of the parks Chris looks after. He didn't say anything about a grave being found out there.'

'I asked him not to,' said Bob. 'We had to get an anthropologist from Adelaide University to determine how old the bones were and help us identify them. Initially, we thought the bones might be part of an indigenous burial site.'

'She was offered a place at Adelaide, you know. Architecture. Came in the post after they'd gone.'

Bob took a sip of his coffee. 'What was she like?'

'She took after her Dad. Intelligent, funny, full of life. Lots of friends.' Sue looked across the table at Bob. 'Do you have any kids?'

'Two girls. Both at uni down in Adelaide.'

'I missed out on that part of her life and everything that would have come after it.' Sue shook her head. 'What happens now?'

'Adelaide will open a murder investigation. I expect they'll want to talk to you.'

'About what?'

'They'll want to talk about what was going on in her life when she disappeared.'

'Again?' said Sue. 'Thought they'd have enough in their files from all the interviews we've had since they disappeared.'

'I'm afraid it's standard practice when a missing persons case transitions to a murder investigation.'

Sue decided there was no point in protesting. The decision wasn't Bob's to make and it probably wouldn't take long. She just didn't feel like going over it again. It wasn't going to change anything.

'What about her remains? Will I be able to give her a proper burial?'

'The Coroner's Office will be in touch when they're ready to release her remains for burial, Mrs Marshall. Probably within the next few days.'

Sue put down her coffee cup. 'Have you spoken to Andrew's parents?'

'My next call,' said Bob, standing. 'This will be public knowledge tomorrow, Mrs Marshall, so you might want to think about how you're going to handle the media attention.'

Memories of reporters with camera teams, showing up to ask questions whenever one of the TV stations decided to run a special on missing persons, surfaced into Sue's awareness. She'd had enough of them as well.

'What do you suggest?'

'Might pay to stay with Chris and Marlie for a few days and don't answer any calls from numbers you don't recognise.'

―――――

Sue watched Bob Davenport climb into the police Toyota Hilux he'd parked in front of her house and drive away. Then, she sank onto the bench on the front veranda and stared into her front garden, not seeing anything that was growing there.

She'd been waiting for this day ever since that Sunday in 1991, when she'd come home from her first real date with Kevin and found the house empty. She thought of Ross Sloane and the years the poor man had put in looking for them after everybody else had given up. She'd have to call him.

Sue had always thought she'd be relieved to know what had happened to Jane and Andrew. She hadn't for a moment believed they'd run away, as so many others had whispered behind her back. But now she knew, she felt like a party balloon slowly losing its air. She sat, staring into space, not knowing what to do or how to feel.

'Are you okay, Mum?'

Sue looked up. Marlie was standing there with four-year-old Chloe. She hadn't even heard them drive up.

'What are you doing here?'

'Bob Davenport called me.'

Sue's tears started as soon as Chloe climbed onto the bench beside her and said, 'I love you, Grandma.'

When they went into the house, Marlie took Chloe into the kitchen and opened her lunch box for her.

Sue went into the lounge and called her sister to break the news before she heard it on the radio.

'He said it will be all over the news tomorrow.'

'That's dreadful, Sue. Are you going to be alright? Do you want me to come over?'

Sue loved her sister but the thought of Anne being in her space controlling everything was more than she could face. 'Marlie's here. I'm going to stay with them for a couple of days. Might be best if you wait until the funeral. Think I'll need your support to get through that.'

'When's that going to be?'

'I'm not sure. I have to wait for them to release the remains, and I want to talk about it with Andrew's parents. I'd like to bury them together.'

'You sure that's wise?'

'Anne, they've been in the same grave together for thirty years. What's there to decide?'

Silence. Anne was obviously thinking about her response.

'Guess you're right. Hadn't thought about it like that.'

'I'll let you know when I've made the arrangements.'

Sue ended the call and joined Marlie and Chloe in the kitchen.

'Do you want something to eat, Mum?'

'Did Chris say anything to you about some bones being found out at Red Banks?'

'Told me he'd found some after all that rain we had,' said Marlie, 'but he wasn't sure how old they were, so he told Bob, who got someone from the university that knew about that sort of stuff.'

Sue sat down next to Chloe and tussled her thick dark hair. It was so different to the blonde hair that had adorned Jane's head at the same age.

'Funny to think they've been out there all this time with Chris looking after them.'

'He wanted to tell you but the police wanted to wait until they knew for sure. He asked me not to say anything.'

Sue liked the way Marlie always stood up for Chris. He'd done the right thing marrying her.

'He did the right thing, Marlie. He's always been good to me.'

CHAPTER 6

PAT AND LINA watched the media conference on the TV screen mounted on the wall in the squad room. Inspector Smith was fronting the media scrum, since he was nominally the Senior Investigating Officer.

'How were they killed?' called a reporter they couldn't see.

'That has yet to be determined,' said Inspector Smith.

'So, how do you know they were murdered?'

Pat nudged Lina. 'This should be interesting.'

Inspector Smith took off his glasses, a look of mild amusement on his face as he gazed at the cameras. For a moment, Pat thought he was going to laugh.

'To the best of my knowledge, young people don't normally bury themselves alive,' said Inspector Smith, holding up his hand to quieten the room, 'but we are dealing with skeletal remains, which I trust you appreciate makes it extremely difficult to determine the exact cause of death.'

'When do you expect to arrest their killer?' called another voice.

'We will do out best to track down their killer,' said

Inspector Smith, 'if that person is still alive, but thirty years is a long time and it may very well be that we will never know who is responsible.'

'Have you spoken to the parents?'

'We have, and they have asked for their privacy to be respected. I trust you will honour their request.' Inspector Smith turned to the media officer standing beside him.

The media officer stepped up to the microphone. 'If anyone has any information or knows of anyone who was involved in the disappearance of Jane Edwards and Andrew White in November in 1991, please call Crime Stoppers using the number now visible on your screen.'

The presentation ended with a display of images of Jane and Andrew, taken from the archive of photographs used over the years to highlight their disappearance.

Pat switched off the TV. 'What did you make of that?'

'He doesn't expect us to solve the case,' said Lina.

'Well, our job is to see if we can,' said Pat. 'Are you up for the challenge?'

'You're enjoying this, aren't you?'

Pat decided to trust her. 'Most people around here think I'm a has been and you're a wanna be. What I'd enjoy is sticking it right up their arses.'

Lina smiled. Pat knew she was in.

'I'll see you in the morning.'

———

They spent the first part of the morning in Inspector Smith's office.

'There's really nothing in these statements apart from a reference to some trouble White had with some of his classmates at school, which was put down to him not being one of the boys,' said Pat.

'What troubles me is what's not in these statements,' said Inspector Smith. 'How can two kids disappear in the middle of Burra without anyone seeing anything?'

'Well, it was in the middle of the night,' said Lina.

'Not necessarily,' said Inspector Smith. 'If you look at this statement from Sally Nelson, she says they left her place around midnight, but what time did the mother get home on the Sunday morning?'

Pat skimmed the statement Sue Edwards had given when she'd reported her daughter missing. 'Ten past eleven.'

'That's an eleven hour window,' said Inspector Smith.

'Yeah, but the mother says there were no signs they'd actually come home that night,' said Pat, 'which suggests they were intercepted somewhere during their walk home shortly after midnight.'

Inspector Smith dropped the folder holding his copy of the statements onto his desk. 'You're going to have to interview as many of these people as possible and see if you can jog a memory or two.'

'In person?' said Pat.

'That would be best,' said Inspector Smith. 'We've got a budget allocation to cover costs for this investigation, so you may as well spend some of it before upstairs decides we're wasting our time.'

They spent the afternoon packing and then travelling to Burra.

It was ten to four on a Tuesday afternoon in December when Lina parked their unmarked Camry outside the Burra Police Station.

'Let's introduce ourselves and then find the motel,' said Pat. 'I think we've done enough for today.'

They went into the police station. There was a young female constable sitting at the desk behind the counter separating the waiting area from the interior of the station. Pat flashed his identification card. 'Detective Sergeant Travers. Your sergeant is expecting us.'

'Sergeant Davenport isn't here at the moment, Detective Sergeant, but he asked me to show you where you can set up.'

She let them through into the interior of the station and showed them into the room usually used for briefings.

Pat realised Port Pirie wasn't wasting any money on station upgrades. The room looked like it hadn't seen a lick of paint since 1991. The furniture was a collection of mismatched pieces that had seen better days. At least there was a window, and he could hear the hum of the air conditioning unit blowing cool air into the building through the vents in the ceiling.

'There are data points on that wall,' said the constable, 'and the loos and the tearoom are down there.' She pointed along the corridor.

'Where's your interview room?' said Pat, 'in case we have to get people to come to us.'

The constable turned around and opened the door behind her. 'It's got all the required AV equipment if you need it, Detective Sergeant.'

Pat wondered what calibre of detectives she'd had to put up with over the years. He knew some detectives looked down their noses at Uniform. He wasn't one of them.

'When are you expecting Sergeant Davenport back, Constable?'

'In the morning. He said he'd be here at eight thirty.'

Pat took out a card with his mobile number on it. 'We're staying at the Burra Motor Inn, and this is DC Palumbo.' He'd almost forgotten to introduce her.

'Lina.'

'Jenny Worth,' said the constable. 'Welcome to Burra.'

———

After checking into the motel and agreeing to join Lina for dinner in the restaurant at six thirty, Pat went for a walk. He followed Burra Creek back towards the centre of town and looked through the trees into the caravan park on the other side of the creek. It didn't appear to have many tenants. He stopped at the skate park and watched a couple of teenage boys working on their technique, before making his way to the Burra Hotel, his intended destination.

There was no-one in the front bar except for a man of about forty washing glasses behind the bar. Pat sat on one of the stools and pulled his credit card out of his wallet.

'What can I do you for, mate?'

'Pint of Super Dry,' said Pat.

Pat watched him lift a cold glass from the fridge and fill it from the Hahn Super Dry tap.

'Here on business?' said the barman, placing his beer in front of him. 'That'll be ten.'

'Business,' said Pat, tapping his card on the EFTPOS machine and thinking his suit was a bit of a giveaway.

'We have a good menu if you're staying long enough to want a bit of variety.'

'I'll keep that in mind,' said Pat. 'We're trying out the Jumbucks Restaurant tonight.'

'Ah, staying at the Motor Inn. They've got a new bloke in their kitchen. Hope he doesn't disappoint you.'

'He'll only get one chance.' Pat started on his beer. 'Been here long?'

'Me? Lived in Burra all my life,' said the barman. 'Been working here for the last six years.'

'What's it like living in a place like this?'

'Quiet, mostly,' said the barman, 'but we see enough tourists to keep us busy.'

'Place has an interesting history,' said Pat. 'Didn't realise they'd found so much copper here.'

'That was way back when. Now it's all about the ruins or people looking for a quiet weekend not too far from Adelaide.'

'Get many grey nomads?' said Pat. 'Saw a caravan park on the way here.'

'Not this time of year,' said the barman. 'See enough of them though.'

Pat noticed the barman's eyes shift their focus to over his left shoulder and looked at the reflection in the glass door of the fridge in front of him. A grey haired man dressed in overalls came in and sat on a stool at the far end of the bar. The barman moved away to serve him.

Pat drained his beer and headed back to the motel to freshen up before dinner. He didn't want to make a fool of himself by turning up reeking of beer.

He hadn't always been a drinker, but after Pam's death he'd gotten into the habit of ending his workday with a pint, sometimes more than that, especially when being on his own really got to him. As he walked back to the motel, he wondered if he had a drinking problem or if he'd be able to control himself and stay sober while they were in Burra. He hoped he hadn't let himself fall too far. He didn't want to end his life as an alcoholic. He'd seen too many others go that way.

Pat joined Lina in the restaurant at six thirty. She'd changed into a skirt and sleeveless top that accentuated her breasts. Perhaps she's testing me, thought Pat, as he sat in the chair opposite Lina at the table and looked at the railway memorabilia displayed around the edges of the room, hoping he'd be able to live up to her expectations of him as a gentleman.

'How was your walk?'

'Just needed to stretch the legs,' said Pat. 'I didn't go far.' He decided to relax and look at her in toto. Her pretty face and ready smile set him at ease. He decided she probably wasn't testing him at all, just being herself with someone she felt comfortable with.

Lina picked up the menu. 'It's quiet here.'

'One of the benefits of country living,' said Pat, running his eyes down the menu. 'Think I'll have the steak.'

'I'm going for the Thai green curry,' said Lina. 'Do you fancy a wine?'

'I don't mind a red,' said Pat.

'We may as well use the allowance,' said Lina. 'How about a bottle of the Lodge Hill shiraz?

'Suits me,' said Pat.

They ordered and sat back to wait.

'Do you have any kids?' said Lina, sipping on her glass of water.

'I have a daughter about your age,' said Pat. 'She's a teacher at Brighton Primary. Took after her mother. And a son. He's in Darwin with the RAAF. Does something technical.'

'See them much?'

'Catch up with my daughter for lunch on Sundays when I can. She lives with her bloke at Hove,' said Pat. 'They bought an old house with one of those huge backyards. Great place for a barbecue.' He took a sip of his water. 'Get to see my son once or twice a year.'

'Darwin's a long way away,' said Lina.

'Yeah, well with this Covid stuff, I haven't seen him in nearly two years, but he calls me most Friday nights.'

'That must be hard.'

Pat smiled. 'What about you? Got a bloke in your life?'

'I've had a few but none of them seem to last,' said Lina. 'Something about the shift work.' She laughed.

'Or being with the police,' said Pat.

'Funny about that. How you'd manage to team up with a teacher?'

'Pam and I were high school sweethearts,' said Pat.

'Like our victims,' said Lina.

Pat hadn't made that connection. 'We had a bit more luck than they did, though. At least we got twenty five years together before she died,' said Pat.

'How long ago was that,' said Lina, 'if you don't mind me asking?'

'It's okay,' said Pat. 'Breast cancer took her five years ago. At least it was quick.'

The waiter arrived with their bottle of shiraz and showed Lina the label.

'Go ahead,' said Lina.

They sat in silence while the waiter poured wine up to the line on their glasses.

'Cheers,' said Lina. 'Here's to success.'

'Yeah,' said Pat. 'You do realise we're going to need all the help we can get to crack this one, don't you?'

Lina winked at him. 'You're the expert, Pat. I'm here to learn.'

'So, what made you get into the job?'

'My grandfather,' said Lina. 'He was in the Carabinieri in Italy before they came to Australia. Told me a lot of stories. Guess I wanted to see if it was anything like he said it was.'

'Hope you weren't disappointed,' said Pat.

'My father was the one who was disappointed,' said Lina. 'He reckons his father was a romantic with all his stories. Said their life in Italy was nothing special, and claimed the real reason they came to Australia was to get away from the Mafia.'

Pat took a sip of his shiraz. 'How old was your father when they came to Australia?'

'Twelve,' said Lina, 'and I gather he wasn't happy about leaving his friends.'

'How come he didn't go back?'

'You don't know much about the Mafia, Pat,' said Lina, with a grin on her face.

'Can't say I've had any experience,' said Pat, 'but I guess you're telling me the sins of the father are inherited by the sons.'

'My grandfather changed his name,' said Lina.

'What? Like in witness protection.'

Lina shook her head. 'No, like in running away and disappearing.'

'Is he still alive, your grandfather? Think I'd like to meet him.'

Lina shook her head. 'Might have run away from the Mafia but couldn't give up the fags. Died of lung cancer not long after I joined the force.'

'Sorry to hear that,' said Pat.

The waiter returned with their meals and topped up their glasses.

'This looks good,' said Pat, placing the serviette in his lap and picking up his fork and knife. 'Hope it tastes as good as it smells.'

CHAPTER 7

SHORTLY AFTER EIGHT thirty on Wednesday morning, Pat and Lina met with Sergeant Bob Davenport at the police station.

'Sorry I wasn't here when you arrived,' said Bob. 'Regional meeting over in Clare.'

'No problem, gave us time to settle in.' Pat looked around Bob Davenport's office. It's drab colours and the faded notices on the wall behind Bob left him feeling depressed. He wasn't worried about the delay in meeting with the local sergeant to get their bearings. Nothing about this investigation had a feeling of urgency. He didn't even think they were going to get anywhere with it, despite what he'd said to Lina.

'Where do you want to start?' said Bob.

'Seeing this is a murder investigation, I guess we'd better take a look at the crime scene,' said Pat, 'although I doubt it will tell us much after thirty years. But it might help to know where it is in relation to where they were last seen.'

'It's a fair way out of town,' said Bob. 'I'll get Jenny to run you out there.'

'Have you spoken to anyone about our investigation?' said Pat.

Bob smiled. 'Who do you think got to break the news to the parents?'

Ah, the joys of being the local sergeant, thought Pat. 'How did they take it? Thirty years is a long time to wait to find out what happened.'

'Told them to expect a visit,' said Bob, 'but I wouldn't plan on them being excited to see you.'

'Do you know them?'

'Had little to do with them in my time here,' said Bob. 'They're in their seventies. It's not like they've come to my attention.'

Pat turned to Lina. 'What was the name of the sergeant who was here when they went missing?'

'Sloane. Ross Sloane,' said Lina.

'I've met him,' said Bob. 'He dropped in for a chat after the news broke. He's retired. Lives in Clare. I've got his details if you want to catch up with him. Reckon he'd appreciate a visit.'

'He's on our list,' said Pat.

⸻

Pat studied the ground in front of them, a depression of disturbed red dirt where the CSI team had backfilled the hole they'd created when exhuming the skeletons. The site was located at the bottom of a gulley about twenty metres from the nearest trail. Day trippers would have to disregard the rules and wander off the marked pathways to stumble across the site of the excavation.

That was probably why the killer had chosen this spot

for the grave, thought Pat, but he still couldn't understand why the killer chose to bury his victims within the conservation park. There were so many other places around Burra he could have used, and a lot of them were existing holes where all he'd have had to do was dump the bodies. Here, in the conservation park, he'd had to dig a grave and then cover up the bodies.

Pat turned to Lina, who was snapping photos of the site and its surrounds with her smartphone. 'This had to be premeditated.'

'What makes you think that?' said Lina.

'The case notes suggest the victims met up with their killer some time after midnight, so I think we can assume the killer wanted to take advantage of the cover of darkness. Right?'

'Yeah, that makes sense,' said Lina.

'There's nothing suggesting they were killed in Burra. In fact, everything points to them being killed here. But why here?'

'You think he'd already dug the grave before bringing them out here?'

Pat swept his arm around pointing at the trees growing on the hillside. 'It's not like there is any easy access, apart from walking up that path over there, and it would be easier to dig their grave in daylight, when you could see what you were doing, don't you think?'

'Wouldn't that be a bit risky?' said Lina. 'After all, this is a public park.'

'Not really,' said Jenny, 'if things back then were anything like they arc now. This is the quiet time of the year. We hardly have any tourists around here over the summer. It's too bloody hot.'

'We're probably dealing with a local,' said Pat. 'Someone who knew this place well enough to know he could dig a hole out here without being discovered.'

''Yeah, well he was right about that,' said Jenny. 'If it hadn't been for all the rain we had last month we still wouldn't know this was where he buried them.'

'Somebody with access to a vehicle of some sort,' said Lina, 'and a twenty-two.'

'That could be every farmer in the district,' said Jenny.

'Or a traveller with local knowledge,' said Pat. 'Someone who'd visited enough times to know the lay of the land.'

'But why these kids?' said Lina. 'If you're right about it being premeditated, it's got to be someone who knew them. Someone who knew where they'd be on the night they went missing.'

'That narrows it down a bit,' said Jenny.

'Yeah, but they all have alibis,' said Pat, 'unless some of them lied.'

'At least we have a starting hypothesis,' said Lina, 'and we can revisit those alibis.'

Pat let himself feel the little glimmer of hope her words inspired, and then brought himself back to reality. A lot of things could happen in thirty years, and lot of things could be forgotten.

On the way back to the police station in Burra, Jenny drove Pat and Lina from 7 Welsh Place, where the book club members had held their end of school year party in 1991, along Paxton Terrace and around to the victim's intended destination at 2 Essex Street. Then they went back to Welsh

Place and drove over the alternate route the victims could have walked along Kingston Street and Pleasant Road.

'What do you see?' said Pat, as they travelled along Pleasant Street towards Paxton Terrace.

'Wide streets, not many lights, houses set back from the street,' said Lina.

'Places where you could intercept someone without anybody knowing, especially over there in Essex Street,' said Jenny, pointing across Paxton Terrace to the vacant land bordering Essex Street.

'This really is the edge of town, isn't it?' said Pat.

CHAPTER 8

AFTER A TAKEAWAY LUNCH purchased from St Just Cafe in Commercial Street and consumed in the shade of the trees along Burra Creek, Pat and Lina drove around to 24 Kangaroo Street to interview Michael and Cynthia White.

Pat wasn't sure what to expect. The file notes told him Michael had been the works manager for the local council and Cynthia a domestic for Burra Hospital when their son disappeared. Given Michael had to be seventy-two and Cynthia pushing sixty-nine, according to their date of birth entries in the file, Pat assumed they were retired now. Not for the first time, he wondered what sort of life they'd endured since their son had gone missing. He couldn't recall meeting anyone who had coped with the sudden exit of a loved one from their life, himself included, and wondered if thirty years would be enough time to heal the wound.

'You okay, Pat?' said Lina, parking in the shade of the tree in front of the house.

Pat saw the concern in her eyes. 'Just thinking. It must have been hard for these guys.'

'Probably still is, and I suspect talking to us won't help,' said Lina. 'Shall we go?'

Pat smiled and opened the car door, relieved not to be facing the Whites on his own. They crossed the gravel driveway and climbed the steps up to the front veranda. Pat pushed the doorbell. They waited.

The door was opened by a tall man with close-cropped white hair, wearing an open neck shirt stretched over a rotund belly straining its lower buttons, cargo shorts, and sandals.

'Mr White?'

'You must be that detective bloke that rang. Call me Michael.' He stepped out onto the veranda. 'I'd shake your hand but we're not supposed to be doing that, are we?'

'Pat Travers,' said Pat, 'and this is my colleague, Lina Palumbo.'

'Come in. It's a lot cooler inside.' He held the door open for them. 'Straight down. The missus is in the dining room down there on the left.'

Pat ushered Lina in and followed her down the dimly lit passageway.

A woman of generous proportions with jet black hair, wearing a knee-length floral summer frock that reminded Pat of his wife's favourite tablecloth, appeared in a doorway on their left. 'Hello, there. I'm Cynthia.'

They sat around the table.

'Hope this is safe distancing,' said Cynthia. 'We're double-vaxxed.'

'This will be fine,' said Pat. 'We've had our jabs.'

'So, what happens now?' said Michael. 'Bob Davenport told us you'd be opening a homicide investigation, but how's that going to work after thirty years?'

'It's not going to be easy,' said Pat. 'Thirty years is a long time and, to be honest, there's no guarantee we'll find out who killed them.'

'What will you do?' said Cynthia.

'Our job is to review the missing persons investigations and speak to everyone again, assuming they're still around, to see if recent events have triggered something in their memories.'

'How's that going to help?' said Michael. 'Surely the statements people made back when it all happened would be more reliable than today's memories.'

'Context affects what people remember,' said Pat. 'When those statements were made, people were thinking about Jane and Andrew as missing persons. Now that it's a murder investigation they may think about it differently and remember things that didn't seem important at the time.'

'Won't change our thinking,' said Cynthia. 'We never thought they'd run away. We've always known they weren't coming home.'

'Why did you think that?' said Lina.

'They had no reason to run away,' said Cynthia. 'They were bright kids with plans, and they had our blessing to follow their dreams.'

'And, they didn't take anything with them,' said Michael, 'not even a change of undies.'

That made sense to Pat. He couldn't imagine them running away from home with nothing unless they'd been desperate to get away, and there was nothing in the file that suggested that would have been the case. 'Any reason they'd go out to Red Banks?'

'Somebody had to have taken them out there,' said Michael. 'They didn't have a car.'

'I was wondering if they'd met up with someone after the party and gone out there,' said Pat. 'You know, an after party with some of their other mates?'

Cynthia glanced at Michael. 'They didn't really have any other friends.'

'Oh, why was that?'

'Andrew was a bit of what you might call a nerd, more into his books and drawing than sport or mucking about with other boys,' said Michael, 'which didn't win him any friends, apart from the girls in his class at school.' He smiled. 'He'd always played with the girls, right from when he was little.'

'And that got him into trouble at school, especially after he and Jane started spending time with each other,' said Cynthia. 'She was very popular and some of the other boys in his class gave him a hard time over it. We had to ask the school to do something about it.'

'Did they?' said Pat.

'Yes, and Ross Sloane followed them up after Andrew and Jane disappeared. That will all be in his report,' said Michael. 'His wife worked at the school.'

'What did you think had happened to them at the time?' said Lina.

'We thought someone passing through must have taken them,' said Michael. 'We get a few strange people around here from time to time.'

'Did you suspect anyone?' said Lina.

'There really was no-one to suspect,' said Cynthia.

'What about the boys that had bullied your son at school?' said Pat.

'Murder is a long way from name calling and a bit of pushing and shoving,' said Michael, 'unless it was a prank that went too far.'

'Don't think it was a prank,' said Pat. 'Jane was shot.'

'What about Andrew?' said Cynthia. 'How was he killed?'

Pat hesitated, wondering how she'd react to what he was about to say. 'We can't be certain, but it looks like he was hit over the head with something.'

Cynthia simply closed her eyes for a moment, and then looked at Michael.

'So, definitely not a prank then,' said Michael. 'That sounds like the action of someone who meant business.'

'I'm afraid so,' said Pat, 'and someone who knew the area well enough to choose Red Banks as the place to hide their bodies. Somebody local, I suspect.'

Michael leant back and crossed his arms. 'You do realise Red Banks wasn't a national park back then, don't you? It was where people from all over hooned around in off-road vehicles making a mess of the place. We had a hell of a job getting the government to protect the place.'

'When did it become a national park?' said Lina.

'In 2002,' said Michael, 'but we got the off-road vehicles kicked out in 1992.'

'Were you involved in that action?' said Pat.

'We signed the petition,' said Cynthia, 'along with everybody else living in Burra, but that was after the kids disappeared.'

'We'll be in touch,' said Pat, standing, 'but, as I said, there are no guarantees we'll find out who did this.'

'We understand,' said Michael, 'but it would be something if you did.'

Michael and Cynthia White stood on their front veranda and watched the two detectives get into their car and drive away.

'Do you think they'll find anything?' said Cynthia.

'He didn't sound all that hopeful to me,' said Michael. 'I suspect they're just going through the motions for our benefit.'

Cynthia turned to go back into the house. 'It's not like it's going to change anything if they find out who killed them, is it? They'll still be as dead as they've always been.'

'You okay?' said Michael. 'They haven't upset you, have they?'

'It's not them,' said Cynthia. 'They're just doing their job. It's just thinking about it. Some days I think we'd have been better off never knowing, and now we know they were buried out there all along, it doesn't make it any easier.'

'At least we know he didn't run away,' said Michael.

'Yes, there is that,' said Cynthia, 'but it doesn't help. I never believed that story in any case.'

'No, me neither.'

Cynthia kissed him on the cheek. 'I'll put the kettle on.'

Michael stood on the veranda after she'd gone inside and looked out across the yard to where the police vehicle had been parked in the shade. He didn't envy them their job. They had an almost impossible task ahead of them, and he wondered how long they'd pursue their investigation before assigning it to the too hard basket. Then, he went inside for a cup of tea.

CHAPTER 9

AFTER SPEAKING to Michael and Cynthia White, Pat and Lina drove across country to Clare in order to interview Ross Sloane, the retired sergeant who'd led the initial investigation when Andrew and Jane had been reported missing.

It was late afternoon when they arrived at the address Bob Davenport had given them, a cottage with a large garden in Opie Street. Ross opened the front door as they stepped onto the veranda. He didn't look like a man of seventy five years, apart from the white hair.

'Good of you to make time for us, Ross,' said Pat.

'Come through to the back,' said Ross. 'Mary's made some afternoon tea for us.'

He led them through to a shaded pergola at the rear of the house, where Mary was placing a tray of small cakes and a teapot next to four fine china tea cups perched in their saucers.

They spent the next twenty minutes on afternoon tea and small talk, finding out about the retired life in Clare.

'Well, we know you're not here to talk about us,' said

Ross. 'So, how can we help with your investigation? I take it you've read my report.'

'Did you ever expect it was anything beyond missing persons?' said Pat.

'Right from the start,' said Ross. 'Mary knew the kids. I knew the parents. That's the way things are in a small town. It just didn't sit right with me that they were runaways, despite what the Port Pirie detectives thought.'

'Why was that?' said Pat, picking up the last of the cupcakes and smiling at Mary.

'They were bright kids,' said Mary. 'Lovely kids. They had big dreams and the grades to go with them. They came from good homes. There was nothing in their lives to run away from.'

'What about the trouble Andrew had with some of the boys at school?' said Lina.

'That was just a bit of rough play, really,' said Mary. 'It stopped as soon as the deputy spoke to them and, besides, it was back in the middle of the year, months before they disappeared.'

'What do you think was behind it?' said Lina.

'Adolescent jealousy,' said Mary. 'Jane was very popular with the boys, and a couple of them didn't take too kindly to her pairing up with Andrew.'

'Why was that?' said Pat.

'Andrew wasn't like the other boys. He wasn't into sport or clowning around. He was the studious type and a gifted artist. They liked it when he drew their portraits, even the crazy caricatures he did for the school magazine, but they weren't happy when it became obvious that he and Jane were a couple. They were all after her, especially John

Grant.' Mary laughed. 'He thought he was God's gift to women, but he was a right royal pain in the arse, very immature, right up until the end of that year.'

'What about the other boys mentioned in the report?' said Lina. 'Paul Maitland and George Young?'

'Paul was John's best friend. They did everything together, including harassing Andrew,' said Mary, 'and George, poor George, he did whatever they told him to, even if it got him into trouble.'

'Did you suspect them of being involved?' said Pat.

'They were at the top of my list,' said Ross, 'but they weren't in town that night. They were at the Grant place, a couple of ks this side of Hanson, having their own end of year celebration, but I only ever had their word for that. The Grants were down in Adelaide and the Youngs said Paul picked up George to take him out there for the night.'

'Weren't spotted in town?' said Pat.

'You been around to Essex Street?' said Ross. 'They could have sat there half the night and nobody would have seen them.'

'Might be worth another look,' said Pat. 'Where are those boys now?'

'John's taken over the family property at Hanson,' said Ross. 'His father had a heart attack a couple of years back and they moved into Clare, a couple of streets from here.'

'His father made him repeat year twelve so he could get into Roseworthy,' said Mary. 'He was a different boy that year. Did very well.'

'I hear he's into something called regenerative agriculture,' said Ross. 'Saw him on Landline a few months back. Bit of a model farmer.'

'What about Paul Maitland?'

'His family has a property north of Burra. Paul manages it with his brother, Philip. Plenty of money there.'

'And, George Young?'

'Last I heard he was living in Peterborough, working out of the council depot,' said Ross, 'but that was a few years ago.'

'Poor George,' said Mary. 'His family had a property in the dry country out past Baldina. They had a string of bad years after George left school. The bank foreclosed. Fred Young shot himself. Left a wife and three kids. George was the oldest.'

'Shotgun,' said Ross. 'Made a hell of a mess.'

Pat didn't want to think about that. He'd seen enough blood and gore at his own crime scenes. 'It looks like one of our victims was shot with a twenty-two. There was a spent cartridge in the grave.'

Ross smiled. 'Every man and his dog has one of those up here. I'd say you had Buckley's of finding that.'

'Would many of them have been handed in during the gun buyback?'

'Not up here, mate. They're a basic farm implement, but they'd all be registered these days. I did licence and safety checks to make sure they were stored properly. I guess Bob still does.'

'But, it's possible a weapon used in 1991 could had evaded all that, isn't it?' said Lina.

'If someone had wanted to keep it hidden or lose it,' said Ross.

Pat put down his empty tea cup. 'I know you searched around Burra, Ross. What about Red Banks? Did you ever look out there?'

'Been out that way?' said Ross.

'Yeah, pretty bleak landscape,' said Pat.

"Gets worse the further out you go and you can go out for a long way.' He looked Pat in the eyes and shrugged. 'Where would you start? We searched all the obvious places around Burra, and some of the not so obvious before I got told to stop wasting my time.'

'Then it just became a media thing,' said Mary.

'Ross, now that you know they were killed, does anyone else come to mind? Any drifters in town around the time?'

Ross Sloane shook his head. 'Burra is a tourist town, Pat, but it's pretty slow around this time of the year, as you've probably noticed. We followed up everybody staying in town that weekend. Nothing. They all had alibis and we couldn't come up with a motive to explain why any of them would want to abduct and kill a couple of local teenagers. It just didn't make sense. Still doesn't.'

'So, what made them declare it a major crime,' said Lina, 'if the investigating detectives thought they were runaways?'

'All the unanswered questions,' said Ross. 'No-one could explain why or how they'd left town or why they'd left every-thing behind and hadn't accessed their bank accounts. In the end, common sense told us something had to have happened to them.'

'Yeah, and I've read that report as well,' said Pat. 'Can't say it helped much.'

Pat stared at the featureless fields of dried grass and wheat stubble as they drove towards Burra, passed through the tiny settlement of Farrell Flat and headed for Hanson.

'Sounds like we're going nowhere if someone doesn't change their story,' said Lina.

'At least we're giving them the opportunity,' said Pat, 'even if they don't take it.'

'You know,' said Lina, 'everyone's assuming they were abducted after they left the party. What if they never left the party?'

'We have several witnesses that say they did,' said Pat.

'But it's like with the boys,' said Lina. 'Three of those witnesses belong to the same family. They're their own alibi.'

'What would be their motive?'

'Haven't got that far,' said Lina. 'Hard to find a motive even for Ross Sloane's suspects. Bit of a jump from school-yard harassment to murder, don't you think?'

Pat thought back to his own high school days. He'd been taken out of circulation not long after he'd started year twelve when he'd met Pam Scone, and she'd decided he was the one. There'd been plenty of lust filled days and macho bravado before she came along, and he'd been involved in a couple of schoolyard scraps with a few of the boys who thought they owned the place. But none of them had gone on to commit murder at the end of the school year.

'Yeah, I wonder whether we're barking up the wrong tree and it was someone from out of town who wasn't staying in Burra,' said Pat. 'I mean how long did it take us to get to Clare?'

'About thirty minutes,' said Lina, 'and Clare's not the only place you can stay around here.'

'We still have a motive problem,' said Pat.

'Well, it's either someone who gets his kicks out of killing kids or someone who wanted to hurt the parents.'

'Or someone who had a specific beef with our victims,' said Pat 'which brings us back to John Grant and his mates.'

The SatNav chirped directions. 'This is the turn off,' said Lina.

***

The Grant homestead, built of local stone, with a wide veranda along its western and northern sides, sat on the northern side of a group of farm buildings surrounded by gum trees that towered above their roofline.

A black kelpie on a chain barked as they entered the yard between the buildings. As they pulled up beside the white Land Cruiser parked in the yard, a man dressed in stained work clothes came out of one of the sheds and waited while they climbed out of the car.

'Mr Grant?' said Pat.

'Yeah, you that copper that called?'

'Detective Sergeant Pat Travers,' said Pat, 'and this is Detective Constable Lina Palumbo.'

John Grant adjusted his hat with his right hand. 'What can I do for you?'

'As I said when I called, we're talking to everyone who knew Andrew and Jane at the time they disappeared to see if the discovery of their remains has triggered memories of anything they didn't tell us at the time.'

'Doesn't change anything as far as I'm concerned,' said John. 'I was here with my mates the night they disappeared.'

'That would be Paul Maitland and George Young?' said Pat.

'Yeah. We were close back then. Guess that's what going to school together does, hey?'

'See much of them these days?' said Pat.

'See Paul a bit,' said John, 'but haven't seen George for years. Lost contact after school really. He moved away when I was at Roseworthy.'

'Yes, Ross Sloane told us about his father,' said Pat.

'Ross bloody Sloane,' said John. 'Gave me a hard time back in the day. Just as well Dad played golf with him.'

'What can you tell us about Andrew and Jane?' said Pat.

John rubbed the back of his neck with his left hand. 'Long time ago. What is it? Thirty years?'

'It is,' said Pat.

'I didn't have much to do with Andrew, really. He was a townie and didn't play sport. Spent a lot of time with the girls at school. Always had his nose in a book. A hell of a lot smarter than me.'

'And, Jane?'

'She was hot,' said John, folding his arms. 'Had one of those personalities. Everyone wanted to be her friend. She was bright too. Probably why she and Andrew got on so well. She didn't have much time for blokes like me, though. We were simple farm boys, as far as she was concerned.'

Pat couldn't detect any emotion in Grant's words, whose answers sounded pretty matter of fact to his ear. 'I understand you were reprimanded for harassing Andrew earlier that year. What was that about?'

'Just boys being boys,' said John, 'and me being a dickhead. It only happened the once. The school told my old man, and that was the end of that.'

Pat wondered about the nature of the relationship between John and his father. 'Bit strict, was he?'

'Didn't take any nonsense,' said John. 'Still doesn't.' John smiled. 'Still thinks he's running the place.'

'Ross told us he'd had some health issues and moved into Clare.'

'Knocked him about a bit but hasn't stopped him interfering,' said John. 'Anything else you want to know?'

'Any thoughts on why someone would want to kill Andrew and Jane?'

'Had a lot of talks with Ross Sloane about that over the years but, like I told him, I have no idea.'

'Did you know about the book club?' said Lina.

John studied Lina's face and stroked his chin with the fingers of his right hand. 'We all knew about the book club but you had to be a girl or Andrew White to join.' He shook his head and laughed. 'They held their bloody meetings when we were playing sport.'

'Did you know the other members?' said Lina.

'I married one of them,' said John. 'Rebecca Owens.'

'Is she around to talk to?' said Pat.

'Not today,' said John. 'She doesn't get home until after nine on Wednesdays.'

Pat handed John his card. 'Get her to give me a call. We'd like to talk to her.'

***

After dinner with Lina in the restaurant, Pat retired to his room and called his daughter to confirm he'd be back in time for Sunday lunch. Something positive to look forward to, he thought, as he ended the call and picked up the TV remote. He flicked through the channels, but nothing caught his interest.

He opened his laptop and read through the report he'd

typed up after they'd returned from the day's interviews. He didn't feel optimistic about solving the case. No-one had changed their story or added any new details that shed light on the murder of Andrew and Jane. They hadn't uncovered anything to justify searching specific properties for a twenty-two rifle that had been in the family since 1991 or before, and he knew starting an area wide search would alert their killer, especially if he was a local and still had the rifle. Then, there was the question of the gun amnesty associated with the 1996 National Firearms Agreement. The perfect opportunity for the killer to dispose of the weapon, thought Pat, and he wondered how many killers his colleagues had assisted during that period.

Then a thought crossed his mind. If the killer had gotten away with it for five years by the time of the gun amnesty, would he feel the need to get rid of the rifle? Did he even know he'd left a spent cartridge behind in the grave?

Pat couldn't see Inspector Smith authorising an extensive or specific search without more details. Pat wrote himself a note. The only way forward with locating the rifle would be to ask Bob Davenport to keep an eye out for an old twenty-two when his team was conducting their licence and gun storage checks, and to arrange for a test firing of any age appropriate rifles.

He leant back in his chair and massaged his temples with his fingers. They didn't have any serious suspects, and there was nothing to back up Ross Sloane's hunch that the murder was in some way connected to the schoolboys who had harassed Andrew some months prior to his murder. Pat had come across his fair share of adolescent thugs who had committed thoughtless acts, including murder, but unless

Paul Maitland and George Young turned out to be vastly different in character to John Grant, he just couldn't see it. There was nothing in the history recorded in the files by previous investigators that suggested the boys were killers.

Pat closed his laptop and decided on an early night.

CHAPTER 10

TEN O'CLOCK, Thursday morning. Lina parked the car in the driveway of 2 Essex Street. Pat gazed at the dwelling and wondered what it would be like living in the same house for fifty years or more. He and Pam had occupied three houses over the course of their twenty five years together, and he'd sold the last one and moved into a two-bedroom apartment shortly after her death. He'd thrown out all of her stuff, much to his daughter's displeasure. He couldn't stand being surrounded by reminders of Pam's absence.

Sue Marshall was obviously made of different stuff. She'd stayed on in the house she'd shared with her daughter and two husbands who had died. As he walked across the lawn to the front veranda, Pat wondered if she'd kept any of Jane's belongings, and if he'd have behaved differently if it had been his daughter and not his wife who had died.

He let Lina do the introductions and followed her down the corridor to the kitchen under Sue's direction.

'Can I offer you a coffee or something?' said Sue, as soon as they were seated.

'Coffee would be nice,' said Lina. 'What about you, Pat?'

'Coffee's fine, thanks.'

Pat looked around the kitchen as Sue fussed over making morning tea. The decor was dated. The curtains faded. The cupboards under the sink were scuffed and marked, suggesting years of collisions involving kitchen implements and shoes. There was a framed photograph of Jane, smiling at the camera in her school uniform, on the middle shelf of the glass-fronted cabinet displaying Sue's collection of cups and glasses, that Pat recognised from the copy he'd seen in their file.

'There you go,' said Sue, placing mugs of coffee on the table in front of them, next to a bowl of white sugar, a small glass jug of milk, and a plate of freshly cooked blueberry muffins.

'I guess this has all been a bit of a shock,' said Pat, stirring a spoonful of sugar into his coffee.

'Bit of a let-down, to be honest,' said Sue. 'I knew they were never coming back, right from the day they didn't come home. Now I suppose we will never know what really happened to them.'

'Oh, I think we know what happened to them, Mrs Marshall, but working out who did it and why might be a bit of a stretch, I'm afraid.'

'Thought you might say something like that,' said Sue. 'Guess a box of bones is not much to go on.'

Pat tried one of the muffins. He missed Pam's homemade cakes.

'Do you have any ideas of your own about who may have killed them?' said Lina.

Sue shook her head. 'They were such good kids. Never caused any trouble. Studied all the time, especially in their senior years.'

'What about those boys that caused trouble for Andrew at school?' said Lina.

Sue laughed. 'Jane reckoned the school over-reacted because they taunted Andrew for being gay. She knew Andrew wasn't gay. She'd been sleeping with him for months. No, they were just boys being boys, especially that Grant boy. He was sweet on her, but he wasn't Jane's type.'

'So he said,' said Pat.

'He ended up marrying Jane's best friend, Becky. They make a good couple. They've got two boys, Jarvis and Simon.' Sue smiled. 'Becky still drops around to see me. She works for her father here in Burra. They're solicitors.'

'How did the school find out about the boys harassing Andrew?' said Lina.

'Oh, one of the teachers, Mary Sloane, the policeman's wife, she overheard them and confronted them. The boys really got into trouble for what they said to her, if you ask me.'

Interesting, thought Pat. It was starting to sound like the direction of Ross Sloane's investigation had been influenced by his wife's opinion of the boys.

'Do you think you'll get anywhere with your investigation?' said Sue.

'Not unless someone comes forward,' said Pat, 'or we locate the rifle that was used to shoot Jane.'

'What sort of rifle?' said Sue.

'A twenty-two,' said Pat.

'Everybody had one of them back then, before Port Arthur. Even we had one for shooting rats in the chook house,' said Sue. 'Jane was a crack shot. Andrew couldn't hit the side of a barn.'

'Do you still have it?'

'No, handed it in during the amnesty. Kevin wasn't keen on having guns about the house.'

'That would be Kevin Marshall, Chris' father?' said Pat.

Sue nodded. 'Poor Chris, finding the skeletons like that.'

'How is he?' said Lina.

'I guess he's lucky he didn't come to live with us until after Jane had gone. He'd only met her a couple of times and he was still a little boy,' said Sue. 'I'd only just started seeing Kevin when it happened, and Chris was living with his mum. He didn't come to stay with us until after we got married.' She looked up. 'He's a nice lad. Married a Filipino girl, Marlie. They have a daughter, Chloe. She calls me Grandma.'

Pat watched the smile spread across Sue's face and nodded to Lina. 'We have a few more people to follow up, Mrs Marshall, and we'll let you know if there are any developments.'

'Thanks for the coffee,' said Lina.

'Thanks for coming to see me,' said Sue. 'I appreciate what you're trying to do for me.'

Lina drove them north on the Barrier Highway towards Mount Bryan, until they reached the intersection where the Goyder Highway branched off to the west. She slowed and turned onto the Goyder Highway. Five kilometres further west they came to a driveway where Paul Maitland sat waiting for them in a Land Rover Discovery that had seen better days.

They stood in a loose formation in front of the Land Rover, in an attempt to maintain social distancing.

'What is it you want to know?' said Paul, after they'd made their introductions.

'As I mentioned when I called,' said Pat, 'we're catching up with everyone who knew Jane and Andrew on the off chance the discovery of their remains may have triggered a memory that might help us work out why they were killed.'

Paul leant on the front of the Land Rover. 'Don't think I can help you there, mate. I didn't know about it when it happened and I still don't.'

'I understand you were with John Grant and George Young the night they disappeared?'

'Yeah, we had a party to wind up the school year at John's place. I picked up George from his place around six. His old man wouldn't let him have the ute. Anyway, it was a booze up. We stayed the night. Didn't know anything about Andrew and Jane being missing until we heard it on the radio that night.'

'What do you remember about Andrew?' said Pat. 'What sort of bloke was he?'

Paul smiled. 'Bit of a nerd. Bit of a girl, really. Bright bastard, though. Wanted to be an engineer of some sort.'

'Would you say you were friends?'

'We were classmates all through school, but I wouldn't say we were friends. He spent most of his time with the girls. Couldn't kick a footy to save his life but he had a wicked sense of humour.' Paul's face lit up with a smile. 'You should have seen some of the drawings he did of the teachers.'

'Would you say he had any enemies?'

'We stirred him a bit, but Andrew was basically a nice kid. Not the type to make enemies.'

'What about Jane?' said Pat.

'She was popular,' said Paul. 'She and John were school

captains. He had the hots for her but she wasn't interested. She was bright, like Andrew. They were always together.'

'See much of George these days?' said Pat.

Paul folded his arms. 'His old man topped himself a few years after we left school. Bank foreclosed on them. They went to Adelaide as far as I know. Haven't seen him since.' He let his arms drop down by his sides. 'Funny how life works out, isn't it?'

You can say that again, thought Pat. 'What can you tell me about Red Banks? Ever go out there?'

'Nah,' said Paul. 'Not when we were at school. It wasn't a national park in those days. It was a place for rev heads, but I've taken the kids out there a few times to the picnic races.' He stood up and moved away from the Land Rover. 'Hard to believe they were buried out there all that time.'

Pat thanked Paul for his time and they drove back to the Barrier Highway, where Lina turned their car north and headed for Peterborough, an hour up the road through a dry and barren landscape that had Pat wondering why anyone would choose to live in such a desolate place.

They found the address in Threadgold Street the woman at the District Council Office had given them for George Young. A fibro house with a dying front lawn and a noisy air conditioner protruding from its front wall. When they knocked, the front door was opened by a skinny teenage girl with a shock of blond hair dressed in a long blue T-shirt.

'Who are you?'

Attitude, thought Pat. 'We're the police. We'd like to talk to George Young. Is he home?'

'You don't look like police.'

'We're detectives,' said Pat, showing her his identification. 'Is your Dad home?'

'He's not my Dad,' said the girl.

'Sorry, my mistake,' said Pat. 'Is Mr Young here?'

An older woman appeared behind the girl. 'It's alright, Talia. I'll handle this.' She looked through the screen-door at Pat. 'Did I hear you say police?'

Pat held up his identification. 'Detective Sergeant Travers. I was told George Young lives here.'

The woman opened the door. 'I'm Sylvia Waters. He's my partner. What's this about?'

'We're investigating the death of a couple of teenagers who disappeared from Burra thirty years ago,' said Pat.

'You mean those kids found in that park that's been on the telly?'

'Yes,' said Pat. 'Andrew White and Jane Edwards.'

'What's that got to do with us?'

'George went to school with them,' said Pat. 'We'd like to ask him if he's remembered anything from that time now that their remains have been found.'

'Really?' said Sylvia. 'I didn't know George was from Burra.'

'Is he here?' said Pat.

'He's having his afternoon snooze. Let me see if he'll talk to you.'

They waited at the door, listening to the rattle of the air conditioner in the wall beside them, until Sylvia opened the door and ushered them into the front room. 'He'll be with you in a minute.'

They heard a toilet flush and a door open and close.

Then a haggard George Young limped into the room with the aid of a walking stick and collapsed into an armchair.

'Sorry to keep you waiting,' said George. 'I'm not as flash as I used to be.'

'Sorry to hear that Mr Young,' said Pat, wondering what his illness was. 'Are you up to answering a few questions about Andrew White and Jane Edwards?

'That's going back a ways,' said George.

'Thirty years,' said Pat.

'Yeah, saw it on the news. Brought back some memories, some I'd rather forget.'

Pat assumed he was referring to his father's suicide and his family's subsequent destitution. 'You made a statement to Sergeant Sloane at the time. Remember that?'

'Bastard was trying to finger me with having something to do with their disappearance.' George made air quotes with his fingers. 'Another one of your pranks gone wrong, George?'

'Why do you think he had it in for you?'

'His wife was one of the teachers. I gave her a hard time. She was a bitch.'

'And, were you known for pranks, George?'

George smiled. 'A few.'

'What about harassing Andrew?'

'That was John Grant, not me. Silly bugger couldn't understand why Jane was screwing Andrew and not him. Anyway, I hear he ended up with Becky Owens. She was more his type.'

'Remember where you were the night they disappeared?'

'Bit hard to forget,' said George. 'Must have been asked that question a hundred times. Spent that night getting pissed at John's place with Paul Maitland.'

Pat looked at George and wondered how many other nights of his life he'd spent getting pissed somewhere. 'Any idea who might have killed them?'

George shook his head slowly. 'I've thought about that a lot over the years. I never thought they'd run away like everyone was saying. They had everything going for them. But, I've never figured it out.'

'What's your prognosis?' said Pat.

'Depends,' said George. 'I'm on dialysis and the waiting list for a transplant.' He shrugged. 'At least they picked it up before it killed me.'

CHAPTER 11

Pat and Lina arrived at the offices of Owens Solicitors in Chapel Street shortly after nine thirty on Friday morning. Rebecca Grant was waiting for them at reception. Pat noticed the sparkling blue eyes behind her face covering, a black cloth mask sporting a colourful indigenous design, and felt them probing his soul.

'This is probably the safest place,' said Rebecca.

'Fair enough,' said Pat.

They sat in the chairs arranged in the waiting space in front of the desk, with Rebecca staying behind the reception desk. 'Are you making any progress? John doesn't think you have much of a chance of getting a breakthrough after all this time.'

'He could be right,' said Pat, 'but that won't stop us trying. What do you remember about that weekend?'

Rebecca leant back in her chair. 'I couldn't believe it at first. I watched them head off from Sally's. My father offered to drive them home, but they wanted to walk. It was a beautiful night. I was a bit envious really, but my parents were a little more protective than Jane's mum. I wasn't allowed to walk home after dark, ever. Then Jane's mum rang on the Sunday. After that there was a search and lots of policemen asking questions, and then nothing, until last month.'

'Do you have any idea who may have wanted to hurt them?'

Rebecca shook her head. 'Jane was school captain. Andrew did cartoons of the teachers and the kids in our class. I've still got the one he did of me. I'd known them since we were little. We all started at Kindy together. They were just a couple of kids with plans to go to uni and make a life for themselves.'

'How did they get on with the other kids at school?' said Pat, thinking there had to be something that set the victims apart. After all, they'd been murdered by someone.

'The boys treated Andrew as if he was one of the girls. It had been like that since primary school, to be honest. He just didn't like the rough and tumble of their life. Of course, he was the only boy in our class who was serious about doing schoolwork, which suited us. Sally, Lydia and I are the only ones that went on to uni out of our class that year. John had to repeat the year to get into Roseworthy. The others started work. Most of them were farm boys. All they wanted to do was work with their dads.'

'Was there anyone in town at the time that gave you the creeps?' said Lina. 'Someone the adults told you to stay away from?'

'Not that I recall,' said Rebecca, 'but there were always strange people around. We get a lot of visitors here, and it's been like that for as far back as I can remember.'

'What were the rumours around town at the time?' said Pat. 'What were people like your parents saying about it?'

'I remember my father saying Sergeant Sloane was

barking up the wrong tree. He was convinced John and his mates had something to do with it, but everybody else thought they'd either skipped town or been kidnapped by some psycho.'

'And, what did you think?' said Pat.

'I knew they hadn't run away,' said Rebecca. 'Jane told me all her secrets. We were like sisters. She'd never have run off without telling me. Besides, she had no reason to run away.'

'Do you keep in touch with the other girls?' said Lina.

Rebecca looked at her hands on the desktop. 'Sally's dead. Car accident.' She looked up. 'Lydia's a doctor. She's married to a doctor in the UK. They live in London. Last time we spoke she was struggling to survive the health system meltdown over there.'

'If you think of anything, Mrs Grant, well, you've got my number.'

When they got back to the police station, Pat logged on and checked the daily update from Crime Stoppers. Nothing. The public had lost interest. There were too many other things to worry about, like the test cricket and the Omicron outbreak threatening to overwhelm the health system.

They'd spoken to the key witnesses and all they'd achieved was to confirm what they knew from the historical case notes. Their investigation might be active but their trail was definitely cold. The one piece of evidence they did have, a .22LR cartridge detonated in 1991, was next to useless unless they could find the weapon used to fire it and connect it to a person with a motive and the opportunity to commit murder the night the victims had disappeared. And, the only way to do that would be to locate and test fire every twenty-two rifle over thirty years old in the state.

Pat knew that wasn't going to happen, not while so many police resources were tied up with Covid restrictions, and not while he didn't have a clear suspect.

He called Detective Inspector Smith and brought him up to date with their investigation.

'Put that in writing, Pat, and get yourself back here.'

'Okay, sir,' said Pat.

He told Lina to pack up and went to see Bob Davenport.

'We're on our way, Bob. Thanks for the hospitality.'

'I'll keep an eye out for your twenty-two, Pat. You never know what one of our random checks might turn up.'

'Thought they'd all be registered by now,' said Pat.

'This is the bush, mate. Things get overlooked. Others get forgotten.'

CHAPTER 12

ON THE SATURDAY after returning from Burra, Pat spent the morning doing his washing. Then he did some grocery shopping at the local supermarket, before sitting down to a fresh bread roll stuffed with smoked ham, tomato and cheese, and a bottle of his favourite shiraz, for a late lunch.

Over the course of the afternoon, he thought about their failure to pick up the trail of Jane and Andrew's killer and emptied the bottle. He knew no-one had expected him to get anywhere with the investigation but that didn't make his failure any easier to accept. If anything, knowing he'd been set up to fail pissed him off, but he wasn't sure what to do about it. After all, he'd spent an enjoyable week away from home with Lina and was looking forward to working with her again.

But, despite the effort they'd put into their investigation, the teenagers' murder remained a mystery to him. He suspected Ross Sloane's initial investigation had been influenced by his wife's opinion of John Grant and his friends, even though the sergeant had widened his investigation to identify everyone who had been visiting Burra over the weekend of the disappearance. The detectives from Port Pirie had interviewed a number of the people Ross had identified but, after reading their report, it was clear to Pat they'd been of the opinion Andrew and Jane were runaways, despite their disappearance being classified as a major crime and what they'd been told by their parents.

It appeared Ross Sloane had been the only one convinced they'd come to harm and to have spent any serious time looking for the bodies, even in his own time, right up until he'd been transferred from Burra.

Pat knew several detectives with a fascination for specific cases but he hadn't come across too many uniformed officers with a similar passion for solving a crime. Must be something about being the local sergeant, thought Pat, as he recalled Bob Davenport's promise to keep an eye out for an unregistered twenty-two with an appropriate pedigree.

He thought about the layout of the town, the time of their disappearance and Sue Marshall's insistence Jane's bed had not been slept in. That suggested they'd been intercepted before they'd reached the house, possibly in Essex Street itself, given its position opposite vacant land on the edge of town. Someone either had to know they'd be on that street or been waiting for them. Pat couldn't imagine a random attack leading to two deaths taking place on a quiet back street of a place like Burra. The psycho theory didn't hold water for Pat. It sounded like a convenient excuse for shutting down the investigation to allow the Coroner to deliver an open finding.

The more he thought about it, the more he was convinced the whole thing had been planned. The question he needed an answer to was: why? Solve that, and he knew he'd identify who had pulled the trigger.

He made himself a coffee. They'd focussed on the teenagers being the target. But what if they hadn't? He couldn't see Sue Marshall, a domestic at the local hospital being a target, unless she had some skeletons in her closet. But, Michael White had held a significant position with the local council. Maybe he'd pissed someone off. Perhaps they hadn't asked the right questions or spoken to the right people. He decided he'd speak to Inspector Smith on Monday morning, to see if he'd allow them the time to approach the investigation from another angle. After all, what did they have to lose?

On Monday morning, Pat got clearance to pursue his new line of investigation. They started with online and database searches, and then moved to the newspaper archives in the State Library. By the end of the day, it was obvious to Pat that Sue Edwards and Michael and Cynthia White had lived unremarkable lives prior to the reported disappearance of their children in November, 1991, after which they'd enjoyed a moment of media fame, before fading back into obscurity.

'We're going to have to speak to people in Burra,' said Lina.

'I'll let Bob Davenport know we're coming,' said Pat. 'You'd better pack for a couple of days in case we have to extend the stay.'

CHAPTER 13

GEORGE YOUNG RESTED in the armchair in the front room of the house he shared with Sylvia and her daughter, staring at the air conditioner as the stream of cool air it generated caressed his overheated body. He took a sip of cold water from the glass Sylvia had placed on the table next to him. He closed his eyes. On the screen of his mind's eye appeared the hour glass that he knew represented the span of his life. There weren't that many grains left in the upper glass waiting to fall. He opened his eyes with a start. If he didn't act now it would be too late. He was running out of time.

George had precious little to show for his forty seven years and, after what the doctor had told him that morning, he doubted he'd be making it to his forty eighth birthday. Depressing to say the least, he thought, as he turned his head and watched Sylvia moving about in the kitchen.

Sylvia had been good to him. She'd taken him in when he'd been an unreliable drunk driving the council garbage truck, and stood by him when his kidneys had failed and forced him to stop work. He'd made her the beneficiary of his superannuation but was painfully aware of the miserable amount he'd managed to accumulate, thanks to his intermittent work history. He wanted to do something more for her, something that would set her up for the years she'd have to survive on her own when he was gone. Somewhere at the back of his mind, a small voice was struggling to make itself heard, whispering a possibility he'd done his best to stay away from for thirty years.

The screen inside his head filled with images he couldn't dislodge. Memories of his childhood on the farm. Memories he'd devoted a shitload of energy and booze to suppressing. Memories that had been triggered by the police visiting and asking questions about his life in Burra.

There was a stream of images, remembered by a terrorised thirteen-year-old boy, of his father hitting his mother and taking his sister, Samantha, into her room and shutting the door. That clip was followed by a screening of his memory of the afternoon he spent with Samantha in the hay shed, when she'd told him what their father had been doing to her, and the threats he'd made to force her to keep it secret. George wiped at his eyes with the back of his hand and shook his head. That memory was too painful.

The poverty they had endured and the lying to everyone about what was happening on the farm were not things George liked to think about. He'd tried to make a go of the place for his mother's sake after he'd left school, and fought with his father to stop him hitting his mother and abusing his sisters. But that life had come to an end the day the letter had arrived from the bank, the letter that let him and his mother know Fred Young had lied to them.

He'd been so angry. He'd busted his guts for years only to be betrayed by his own father. But, that day had generated a memory he didn't want to deal with, a memory that was giving him nightmares again. The memory of the night he and his mother had plied his father with whisky and taken him out behind the implement shed, and blown his head off with the shotgun.

Ross Sloane had known it wasn't suicide but that was how he'd treated it. He'd known about Fred Young all along, and had told his mother how to make it look like her husband had shot himself after going on a bender. His mother had called Ross in the morning, and he had come out and made sure the scene was clear before reporting it as a suicide. George had never liked the policeman who had given him a hard time over the disappearance of Jane and Andrew, but he'd had a grudging respect for him after what he'd done for his mother.

When the bank had finally foreclosed on the farm, his mother and sisters had started life again down in Adelaide. George hadn't been able to face his sisters after what he'd been unable to stop their father from doing to them. He'd gone north, and been on the run from himself ever since.

But that wasn't the memory that was whispering to him about how he could repay Sylvia and set her up for life. Thinking about it aroused him in ways he hadn't experienced for some time. He played with the possibilities and decided, given his circumstances, he had nothing to lose. They couldn't take anything more away from him now that the sands of time were running out for him, regardless of what he did. He made the decision and started thinking about how he could pull it off without alerting Sylvia. He knew she wouldn't want the money if she ever found out what he'd done to get it for her.

He picked up the glass from the side table and took

another swig of the water, and smiled. He'd kept their secret all these years. There was no need for anyone to know besides those who already knew, and he was banking on them wanting to keep it that way.

CHAPTER 14

AFTER SPENDING a couple of hours talking about himself and life in general on their drive back to Burra, Pat was starting to feel comfortable being with Lina. She had a quick sense of humour and a way of setting people at ease, himself included, when she was asking questions. He realised she'd done an excellent job of getting him to open up and tell her things he'd hadn't told anyone, apart from Pam. Too bad he wasn't ten years younger, he thought, as they parked outside the police station. She was attractive in all those ways that made it hard for a man to keep his mind on the job.

They touched base with Bob Davenport and then drove around to Kangaroo Street to interview Michael and Cynthia White again. They sat outside around a table in the shade of the glory vine growing on the pergola at the rear of the house. It was a twenty five degree day, cool for the time of year, but pleasant enough for being outside where it was easier to maintain social distancing, and safe enough to talk without wearing masks.

'Want to explain what you meant on the phone?' said Michael.

'We're taking a look at what happened from another angle,' said Pat. 'To date, we've assumed that Andrew and Jane were not only the victims but also the targets of the crime. In other words, someone set out to murder them for a reason that had to do with them.'

Michael nodded. 'Okay, I get that, but you're thinking there might be another reason?'

'I don't know if there is,' said Pat, 'but I'd like us to canvas the possibilities to see if it takes us anywhere.'

'What other reason?' said Cynthia.

'To get at either or both of you, or Jane's mother,' said Pat.

The Whites exchanged glances. The looks on their faces told Pat they weren't sure where he was going with his new line of enquiry.

'Take your minds back to the late eighties, early nineties. What were you involved in that might have been a little controversial or attracted some opposition from other members of the community?'

Cynthia smiled. 'Oh, we've always been involved in community groups, Pat. They don't usually create conflict, well nothing beyond disagreements about trivial things.'

'What sort of groups?' said Lina.

'For the last ten years or so we've been involved with The Friends of Burra Railway Station. We've restored the station and opened it as a B and B,' said Cynthia. 'Lots of working bees and fund raising mainly.'

'Looks great, by the way,' said Pat. 'We had a look at it last week when we were here.'

'We've turned it back into a community asset,' said Michael. 'You couldn't let a building like that become a ruin.'

'Were you in a similar community group back in the early 1990s?' said Lina.

'The main thing we were doing back then was trying to get the off-roaders out of Red Banks to stop them destroying the place,' said Michael. 'In fact, we were on the organising committee to make that happen and petition the government to turn it into a national park.'

Pat looked at Michael. His face changed. He stared wide eyed at his wife.

'Shit! Do you think that could be it?'

Pat glanced at Lina, and gave his head a slight shake, hoping she'd get the message. She winked at him. They were good.

'There was some pretty vocal opposition to that until the community swung in behind it, now that I think about it,' said Cynthia.

'Do you remember anyone in particular?' said Pat.

'Dan Black, the bloke that ran the Commercial Hotel,' said Michael. 'He was making a killing selling booze to the clowns that came up to drive all over the place. Dan's one I remember, but you're a bit late if you want to question him. He died back in 2010.'

'Did he ever make any threats?' said Lina.

'No, just a lot of noise at town meetings,' said Michael. 'He wasn't the only business owner against closing the place down, but most of them signed the petition when they realised they weren't going to go broke and got a better appreciation of the significance of the place, and its potential value as a national park.'

'Anyone else make trouble over shutting down the park to off-road vehicles?' said Lina. 'Anyone from out of town, for example?'

'There were a couple of car clubs that lobbied to block the petition, but they didn't make any threats,' said Cynthia.

'Anybody else locally?' said Pat. 'I'm inclined to think it was a local when I think about where they were forced into a vehicle and the choice of Red Banks as the place to bury them.'

Michael drummed his fingers on the table. 'The only other person who voiced any opposition was Ross Sloane, which was a bit of a surprise given the number of serious accidents out there, but I reckon he got his monthly quota of tickets booking the blokes who came up to drive around in the park.'

He'd certainly have the local knowledge required, thought Pat, and he'd gone out of his way trying to pin the disappearance on three local lads his wife didn't like. He'd need to find out more about Sergeant Ross Sloane.

'Hardly motive for a double murder, though, said Cynthia, 'besides, he signed the petition not long after the kids went missing.'

Pat scratched his head. It felt like they were clutching at straws. 'What about anything to do with your work?'

'I was responsible for road and streetscape maintenance back then,' said Michael. 'People complained to council, not me.'

'What about you, Cynthia?' said Lina.

'Sue and I were working in the kitchen at the hospital, and doing the cleaning in the old folks section.' She laughed. 'The only people I remember threatening us all had dementia.'

'The only groups I was involved in were the netball and tennis teams Jane played for,' said Sue Marshall. 'Can't imagine anybody wanting to hurt me, Sergeant. I was a nobody working at the hospital. Now I'm a retired nobody no-one worries about.'

Pat thought she was probably right. 'Did you have anything to do with getting Red Banks declared a national park?'

'I signed their petition,' said Sue, 'but that was after Jane disappeared.'

'Thanks for making time to speak to us, Mrs Marshall.' Pat stood and indicated to Lina he was ready to go.

'By the way,' said Lina, getting out of her chair in Sue Marshall's kitchen, 'what did you think of the way Sergeant Sloane handled the investigation?'

Sue smiled. 'He was the only one who believed they hadn't run away. He spent years trying to find them. I felt sorry for him. He was always so apologetic that he'd never found them.'

It was time to go and speak to the sergeant, thought Pat, as they made their way out to their car.

———

Ross Sloane was a little surprised to see them again. 'Thought I'd seen the last of you, Pat.'

'Just covering another angle,' said Pat.

They sat on chairs arranged around the small white table on Ross' front veranda.

'What angle is that?' said Ross.

'Did you ever think anyone else might be the target?' said Pat. 'Say one of the parents, for example?'

Ross shook his head. 'Always thought it had to be some-thing about the victims. Besides, no-one had threatened any of the parents that I was aware of.'

'What about you, Ross? Anyone threaten you? Anyone around that wanted you out of town?'

Ross laughed. 'I'm sure there were people who wanted me out of town but no-one ever said so to my face.'

'What about George Young?' said Pat. 'He didn't seem to have too high an opinion of you.'

'Yeah, well young George was a bit of a lad,' said Ross. 'One of the few locals to cause me any grief, but I only ever had words with him. Pretty tough home life. His mother needed him at home, not in the lockup.'

'Why was that?' said Lina.

'Protection,' said Ross. 'I couldn't get her to press charges against her husband but I'm pretty sure Fred was hitting her.'

'Why didn't you charge him yourself?' said Pat.

'It's complicated,' said Ross. 'There were three kids, including a couple of girls, and Fred was the only breadwin-ner, if you could call what he was earning from his place an income.'

Pat decided there was nothing to gain from making Ross feel guilty about something he had obviously given some thought to at the time. 'Do you remember there being any trouble about the move to get off-roaders out of Red Banks?'

Ross folded his arms and rested his elbows on the table. 'There was a bit of noise at a couple of town meetings, mostly from business owners making money from the clowns hooning around out there.'

'What about Dan Black?' said Pat.

'How do you know about Dan Black?'

'Michael White mentioned him.'

'Dan was one of those blokes that liked the sound of his own voice, besides, he would have had to pay someone to dig the hole for him out at Red Banks. Heart problems,' said Ross. 'I went to his funeral ten or so years ago.'

'And, what about you, Ross? Heard you weren't all that keen on the off-roaders losing access.'

Ross smiled. 'Michael tell you that as well?'

Pat nodded.

'They were my best revenue source by far, and they gave my team all the training they needed on setting up speed traps and getting people to blow in the bag.'

Pat couldn't imagine Ross confessing to that when he'd been in uniform. 'So, how were your constables deployed on the night Jane and Andrew went missing?'

'Deployed?' said Ross. 'Ever done any country policing, Pat?'

'Not me,' said Pat, 'did my time in uniform at Port Adelaide. Everything ran twenty-four-seven.'

'It's a bit different out here in the bush, especially in a place like Burra. There was only the three of us. We only patrolled on a Saturday night if there was some event on that would attract a crowd,' said Ross, 'like grand final night or a community festival.'

'Didn't know Burra had festivals,' said Pat.

'Well, nothing like Adelaide,' said Ross. 'Anyway, the night they disappeared there was nothing on. November's always quiet. I closed the station late afternoon and put the phone on redirect, which meant any calls to the station number went through to Operations, who'd give me a call if anything was urgent, which is what happened on the Sunday.'

'So you would have been home when Jane and Andrew left the party?'

'That was around midnight according to Sally Nelson,' said Ross, 'I'd been home with Mary and the kids, since around six. Reckon I would have been in bed by then. Don't recall there being anything on the telly to keep us up.'

'And, who would have known no-one was patrolling around town?'

'Everybody in town,' said Ross. 'Our routine wasn't a secret, and it wasn't like Burra was a hot bed of crime at the time.'

'Fair enough,' said Pat, 'I guess I would have done the same.'

After their discussion with Ross Sloane, Pat decided they were getting nowhere and it was time to head back to Adelaide and tell the boss they hadn't unearthed anything to work with.

'Do you think we should speak to the detectives that worked on the case?' said Lina, as they drove out of Clare.

'I don't think they even thought about homicide,' said Pat, 'and besides, they're no longer around to talk to. Gone to that retirement village in the sky.'

'I guess that means this will go back to being a cold case until something or someone crawls out of the woodwork with some item of interest.'

'Guess we'll have something else to think about tomorrow,' said Pat, hoping Inspector Smith would continue to let him work with Lina. He gazed out at the countryside, amazed at how different this country, half an hour west of Burra, was from the country half an hour east of the town. It was as if they'd visited two different countries in their tour of the mid-north.

CHAPTER 15

Sᴜᴇ Mᴀʀsʜᴀʟʟ ᴀʀʀɪᴠᴇᴅ at Michael and Cynthia White's for dinner with a cold bottle of sparkling chardonnay.

Cynthia had made her signature dish: crumbed veal cutlets, roast potatoes, and a tossed green salad, which suited Sue. She'd given up eating what she considered fancy food when she'd retired. She couldn't see the point of a woman living on her own going to all that trouble and, besides, her income wasn't what it had been when Kevin had still been alive and wanting to be fed every night.

Michael opened the bottle she'd brought and poured them each a glass of the sparkling wine they all still thought of as champagne, despite the French with their claims of uniqueness.

'Here's to better days!' said Cynthia, raising her glass.

They clinked glasses and took sips of the effervescent liquid.

'What do you make of those detectives who were up here asking questions?' said Michael, as they took their seats around the table.

'Nice enough people,' said Sue, 'but I don't think they have any more idea about what happened than we do.'

'I thought they were clutching at straws when they asked about what we'd been involved in back then,' said Cynthia, serving the cutlets. 'Help yourself to the salad, Sue. It's already got the dressing on it.'

They served themselves from the dishes holding the roast potatoes and tossed salad.

'Would you like some bread?' said Cynthia, offering Sue the basket of warmed slices she'd wrapped in a cotton serviette.

'Thanks,' said Sue, taking a piece from the basket. She waited while Cynthia passed the basket to Michael, then buttered the piece of bread she'd chosen and placed it on the plate next to her cutlet. 'You know, there are days when I wish they'd never been found.'

'It hasn't been easy,' said Cynthia. 'I thought I'd put it all behind me but it's all just bubbled up to the surface again, like it only happened yesterday.'

'Know what you mean,' said Sue. 'You'd think after all the talking about them we've done over the years it would be like visiting an old story we'd heard a thousand times.'

Michael put down his knife. 'Trouble is, the ending's changed. It was all supposition before. Now it's concrete. Now we know they're dead and have been all along.'

Sue took a sip of her bubbly. 'I never once thought they'd run away, Michael. Ask Cynthia.'

Michael looked at his wife.

'She's right,' said Cynthia. 'I couldn't believe it either, but as long as they hadn't been found there was at least some hope.'

'I lost all hope years ago,' said Michael, 'but I'd still like to know who killed them.'

They sat in silence, eating and thinking thoughts they weren't brave enough to voice.

'Guess we're going have to let that go, too,' said Sue. 'It doesn't look like the police have any idea who did it.'

'If Ross Sloane was right,' said Michael, 'it was someone who's possibly still living around here.'

Cynthia topped up their glasses. 'Be terrible if it was.'

'What do you mean?' said Michael.

'Think about it. That would be someone we know,' said Cynthia. 'How would you feel if you found out one of those boys they went to school with did it?'

'You mean someone like John Grant?' said Sue.

Michael drained his glass. 'He was one of the one's Ross suspected at the time.'

'I think Ross was chasing shadows,' said Cynthia. 'Can you see him being a murderer?'

Michael shook his head. 'Certainly not the John Grant we know today.'

'And who were the others Ross suspected?' said Cynthia.

"Paul Maitland and George Young,' said Sue, 'but I could never see it. They were only schoolboys when it happened.'

'I always thought Ross had it in for the Young boy,' said Michael. 'I wonder what became of him after his father shot himself.'

'Family went down to Adelaide, didn't they?' said Sue.

'That's the story,' said Michael.

Cynthia collected the plates. 'Cup of tea?'

They sat around the table looking at their empty tea cups.

'So, how are we going to do this?' said Michael. 'Fishers have already picked up their remains from Adelaide.'

'I guess there's no rush,' said Sue, feeling a little apprehensive about the final closure the funeral would bring.

'We've spoken to Father Aiden,' said Cynthia. 'He's agreed to hold a service for us in St Mary's.'

'He did Kevin's funeral,' said Sue, 'but he doesn't know the kids.'

Michael smiled. 'We'd have to get Father Martin back for that.'

'God, he'd be a hundred by now,' said Cynthia, laughing.

'I'm pretty sure he's dead,' said Sue, 'so Father Aiden it will have to be. I'd like to keep it private. You know, just us and the people that knew them.'

Cynthia looked at Michael and nodded. 'We were thinking the same. We don't want the media turning this into a circus.'

'The Covid restrictions should help us there,' said Michael.

'I'd like to bury them together,' said Sue.

'Can't see why not,' said Michael. 'They've spent the last thirty years in the same grave. Be a shame to split them up now.'

'Fine by me,' said Cynthia.

'When?' said Sue.

'Father Aiden suggested next Wednesday,' said Cynthia. 'That should give us enough time to let people know and put the service together.'

'I'll confirm that with Fishers tomorrow,' said Michael.

'I've got some ideas,' said Sue, thinking back to the two funeral services she'd already organised. 'I'm sure Father

Aiden will give them a good send off once he's heard our stories about them growing up.'

Cynthia collected the tea cups and took them over to the sink.

'I wonder what life's going to be like after this,' said Sue.

'What do you mean?' said Michael.

'It feels like closing the last chapter of a book you don't want to end.'

'I think you still have a few chapters to go yet, Sue,' said Michael.

'I hope you're right,' said Sue, glancing at the clock on the wall. 'Gosh, is that the time. I'd better get myself home.'

CHAPTER 16

JOHN GRANT SAT with Rebecca two pews behind Michael and Cynthia White. He looked around the once familiar interior of St Mary's, the church his parents had attended right up until they'd retired and moved to Clare. John still didn't understand why his parents hadn't retired in Burra, but he'd learnt a long time ago that questioning his father's decisions was a pointless exercise.

Sitting in the pew across the aisle from the Whites was Sue Marshall, along with her stepson Chris and his wife and daughter, and an older woman John didn't know but who looked like she might be Sue's sister.

Behind the Marshalls, sat Ross Sloane and his wife. They'd aged since he'd seen them last. He guessed they'd have to be in their seventies by now. He'd never liked Mary Sloane. She'd caused him nothing but grief during his school days, except for his final year when he'd knuckled down to the task of getting the results needed to get into Roseworthy and keep his father happy.

He looked at the two pinewood boxes sitting on their

biers in front of the altar and remembered why they were there.

There were several people he didn't recognise in the small group that had gathered to farewell Jane and Andrew. He was disappointed that Rebecca was the only member of the book club present, but they'd been to Sally's funeral and he knew Lydia was in London. He spotted Paul Maitland and his wife, Lorna, sneaking in at the last moment.

John didn't pay much attention to the priest or what he was saying. There wasn't much he didn't know about the lives of Jane Edwards and Andrew White. They'd all started school together and been in the same class all through their schooling at Burra Community School. The only one of the gang, apart from Sally and Lydia, who hadn't turned up for the funeral was George Young.

John wondered what had become of George. He hadn't had any contact with him since George had moved away after his father had shot himself. He didn't even know if he was still alive.

The priest gave the final blessing and then the biers holding Jane and Andrew's remains were rolled down the aisle to the porch of the church, where grey suited men from Fisher Funerals transferred them into the back of the hearses parked in front of the building.

Once outside the church, the mourners waited in the sunshine behind their face masks. Paul Maitland walked over to John and elbow bumped him. 'We need to talk, mate,' said Paul, 'but not here.'

John looked at him and raised an eyebrow.

'George,' said Paul.

John wondered what that might mean but didn't get the

opportunity to ask as Ross Sloane and his wife joined them. 'Well, look who we have here.'

'Hello, Sergeant Sloane,' said Paul. 'Haven't seen you in a while.'

'I'm retired these days, Paul. You boys remember my wife?'

'Mrs Sloane.'

'Where's George?' said Mary Sloane. 'I thought he'd be here.'

'Haven't seen him in years,' said John. 'Don't even know if he's still with us.'

'Oh, he's still around,' said Ross. 'The last time I saw him he was working for the Peterborough Council.'

'When was that?' said Paul.

'A couple of years ago,' said Ross, 'bumped into him at the Heritage Rail Centre in Peterborough on one of our day trips.'

'We must look him up,' said John, wondering why Paul wanted to talk about George after all these years.

'Looks like they're ready to leave for the cemetery,' said Paul.

The following day, after Rebecca had gone to work, John called Paul Maitland on the house phone. He had a mobile phone but old habits died hard in his world.

Lorna answered and told him to try Paul's mobile as he was out moving sheep between paddocks.

John took his mobile out of his pocket, found Paul's number, and made the call. While he waited for him to answer, he wondered why Paul had wanted to talk about George.

'Paul Maitland.'

'It's John. You wanted to talk?'

'We've got a problem,' said Paul. 'George wants half a million dollars.'

'What?'

'Says he'll spill the beans to that detective who was up here asking questions if we don't give it to him.'

That didn't make any sense to John. George was as guilty as they were. In fact, the whole thing had been his idea. What was he playing at after all this time? 'When did he call you?'

'Morning of the funeral. His mother heard about it and suggested he attend.'

They both knew George hadn't followed his mother's advice.

'Did he give you a deadline?' said John, wondering how long they'd have to figure out a way of stopping George from doing something stupid.

'Friday, next week.'

'That doesn't give us much time,' said John.

'I guess that's the idea,' said Paul.

John walked out onto the back veranda, attempting to escape the feeling of the house closing in on him. 'I don't know about you, Paul, but I don't have that kind of money sitting around and, even if I did, there's no way I could move it without Becky finding out.' And, John knew that would open a bucket of worms he'd prefer not to deal with, since it was his wife's financial management that was keeping the farm afloat.

'Don't know where George got the idea we'd have that

sort of cash to hand over,' said Paul. 'I'd be lucky if I could get my hands on twenty grand by next Friday without having to talk to the bank, and you know what they're like. Want to know what you want the money for and when you're going to pay it back. Besides, what would I say to Phil?'

John took a deep breath in. He had no intention of handing any cash over to George Young, even if he'd had a way to find the money. He'd read enough to know blackmailing someone was akin to creating a black hole your victim would never escape from. As far as he was concerned, it was better not to become that victim in the first place.

'We need to talk to George. Find out what his problem is,' said John. 'Can't see what he hopes to gain by this. Are you sure he isn't just having a lend of us?'

'Thought did cross my mind,' said Paul, 'but why now?'

'Maybe it was them being found,' said John. 'You know what a sick bastard he could be.'

'What do you want to do?'

'Let's set up a meeting with him. We can at least catch up and see if we can find out what he really wants.'

'Okay, I'll give him a call and set up a meeting, and send you the details.'

John ended the call and sat on the edge of the veranda. It had to be one of George's sick jokes. If he told the police what really happened the night Jane and Andrew went missing they'd all spend the next twenty five years in prison. Then there was Becky to think about. He couldn't see her standing by his side if the truth came out. And, what would the kids think?

Realising they'd have to find a way to silence George if he wasn't joking, John stood and walked across the yard to the implement shed, where he'd hidden the rifle under the workbench at the rear of the shed thirty years ago.

John parked the Land Cruiser in front of the Railway Hotel in the main street of Peterborough. It was an impressive building that had been serving the locals since 1891, when the town had been known as Petersburg and been an important railway junction, not the sleepy historical town now servicing the local agricultural and tourism industries.

John and Paul alighted from the dust covered Toyota and made their way into the Sports Bar, pausing briefly at the entrance to complete the Covid QR check-in procedure using their mobile phones.

George was seated at a table in the far corner of the Sports Bar, away from the bar and the entrance to the restrooms. They walked over and shook hands, despite the Covid protocols. They hadn't seen each other in over twenty five years.

As he pulled out a chair and sat down, John thought George looked like shit behind his face mask. 'You okay, mate?'

'Been better,' said George. 'Don't worry. It's not Covid.'

John and Paul ordered beer along with their chicken fillet burgers. George settled for a lemon squash.

'Off the beer, mate?' said Paul.

'Kidneys are shot,' said George. 'Nurse in the dialysis unit goes troppo if she hears I've had a beer.'

'So, why did you suggest the pub?' said Paul.

'You get over it,' said George. 'Besides, I like to watch the horses.' He pointed at the big screen TV behind the bar. 'So, what's life like in Burra these days? Same old shit?'

'It's changed a bit since you left,' said John. 'Become more of a tourist destination.'

'I hear they turned Red Banks into a national park,' said George.

'Yeah, not that it's made much difference to us,' said Paul. 'It's not like we need to go out there to see what the country looks like.'

The waitress arrived with their drinks.

'So, what have you been doing with yourself all this time?' said John, picking up his glass.

'Went up north to Darwin for a few years after the old man shot himself,' said George, 'but couldn't hack the humidity in the wet. Drifted south over the years and ended up here about ten years ago.'

'We saw Sergeant Sloane at the funeral,' said Paul. 'He told us you were working for the council up here.'

George watched the waitress making her way to their table carrying three plates holding their burgers and waited while she placed a burger in front of each of them. 'Thanks, Margie.' He watched her walk back towards the kitchen. 'Yeah, I was driving the garbage truck, but that was before this happened. I'm buggered now. Don't have the energy to work these days.'

They spent a few minutes in silence, eating burgers.

John wondered whether George's threat was a sign he was desperate for cash. 'You on workers compo, George?'

George shook his head. 'It's not work related, is it? I'm on Job Seeker. It's the only support I can get.'

'That must be tough,' said John. 'Becky says it's a pittance.'

'Becky?' said George. 'Not Becky Owens by any chance?'

John smiled. 'Yeah. I married her.'

'Well, fuck me,' said George. 'I didn't see that one coming.'

'Are you that cut off from the world of Burra?' said Paul.

'Yeah, and who did you end up with?' said George, looking at Paul.

'A girl from Booborowie,' said Paul. 'I doubt you'd know her. I met her well after you'd left the district.'

'Is that who answered the phone when I called?'

'Yes, she runs the homestead and keeps us all in line,' said Paul. 'What about you? Did you ever get married?'

'Nah, not my thing,' said George, 'not after the way my parents treated each other.'

'So, you're living here on your own?' said John, glancing at Paul.

'Yeah,' said George.

'Do you keep in touch with your sisters?'

'Nah.'

'What about your mum?'

'She rings me every now and then,' said George. 'Nothing's been right with us since my dad made a mess of everything.'

John finished his beer and picked at the last of his chips with his fingers. 'So, what's the story with the five hundred grand?'

'I'm broke,' said George, smiling. 'Thought you boys could help me out.'

'Five hundred grand is a bit steep,' said John. 'It's not like either of us has that sort of money under the bed.'

George leant back in his chair and surveyed the room.

They were the only ones eating in the Sports Bar. Everyone else was sitting at the bar watching the horse racing on the big screen. 'You boys have assets. I'm sure you could raise that sort of money without too much trouble.'

'Maybe,' said John, 'but it's not as easy as you think. It's not like we don't have people to explain things to.'

'Not my problem,' said George.

'You do realise you'd go down with us if you told anybody what happened?' said John.

'Yeah, well that doesn't bother me,' said George. 'You'll get twenty years. I don't have that luxury. I'll be lucky if I get to the end of the year.'

John looked at Paul. It was worse than they'd imagined. George was telling them he had nothing to lose, while they had everything at stake. Paul stroked his chin with the thumb and fingers of his right hand. 'So, why that much money?'

'I want to go out in style,' said George. 'I'm sick of being the loser. I deserve at least one good year before I kick the bucket.'

John glanced at Paul again. They had the information they wanted. Paul nodded. 'Half a million bucks is out of the question, George, but we can probably manage something to help you.'

'Like what?'

'Like a few grand a month to make your life more comfortable.'

George crossed his arms and rested them on the table. 'You're not taking me seriously, are you? You think I won't do it.'

'We hear you, George,' said John. 'We're offering to do what we can.'

'We're happy to help you, mate,' said Paul, 'but we have

to be realistic about what we can do, what we can get away with without our partners finding out.'

'I'm tired,' said George. 'This is all getting too complicated. It's doing my head in.'

'Why don't you sleep on it?' said Paul.

George's head drooped. John thought he was going to fall asleep on them. 'You okay to drive, mate?'

George jerked up. 'Drive? Stopped driving months ago. No, one of the neighbours will come and get me.' He took his mobile phone out of his pocket and placed it on the table. 'She's expecting me to call. She drove me down here.'

'We can drop you home, George. That won't be a problem.'

'That's kind of you,' said George, slipping his mobile back into his pocket.

CHAPTER 17

PAT AND LINA were working on the periphery of the taskforce reviewing a number of drug related deaths that had been initially treated as suicides. The taskforce, created after the findings of a recent homicide investigation suggested some of the deaths may have been staged to look like suicides, was being led by a Chief Superintendent. Inspector Smith's team was a small component of the team assigned to the investigation.

In a way, it was like working on any other cold case, however, their role had been restricted to reading statements, trolling through case notes, and joining dots for the lead investigators. Hack work was what Pat called it. But someone had to do it to generate the leads to be pursued by the investigators in the field.

At least Inspector Smith had decided to keep Lina under Pat's supervision for the foreseeable future. Working with her was certainly an improvement on working on his own or with some of the other young detectives looking to make a name for themselves.

Pat's mobile phone pinged, indicating an incoming message. He checked the screen. The message was from Bob Davenport. Opening the message, he wondered if Bob had located the rifle used to kill Jane Edwards, but the message was about George Young being reported missing by Sylvia Waters.

Pat showed the message to Lina. 'What do you think that might mean?'

Lina studied the text of the message. 'Maybe he's gone off to die on his own.'

'What? Do the noble savage thing?'

Lina shrugged. 'He was pretty crook when he spoke to us.'

'Didn't strike me as the type,' said Pat, 'but, hey, I've been wrong before.'

'Why don't you ring Sergeant Davenport and get the details?' said Lina.

Pat made the call. Bob Davenport told him George Young had last been seen leaving the Peterborough Hotel with two men he'd had lunch with on the Friday of the previous week and that his partner had reported him missing when she hadn't been able to contact him on his mobile phone after he didn't come home or call her to come down and collect him.

'Do you know who he had lunch with, Bob?'

'John Grant and Paul Maitland,' said Bob. 'They reckon they went to see him after he didn't show for the funeral of their classmates and they found out he wasn't well. Claim they dropped him off at his house in Threadgold Street around two, on their way home.'

'That's three days ago,' said Pat. 'He told us he was getting dialysis several times a week.'

'That's why his partner is concerned,' said Bob. 'He won't last long without that treatment.'

'Keep us in the loop, Bob,' said Pat. 'That's an interesting development.'

Pat ended the call and told Lina what Bob had told him.

'What are you thinking, Pat?' said Lina.

'Strange they'd get together after the funeral,' said Pat. 'They all told us they hadn't seen each other in years.'

'Maybe the funeral prompted them to catch up,' said Lina. 'You know what it's like at funerals. All that talk about past times, missing friends. At least, that's what I've noticed.'

'You could be right,' said Pat, 'but why would he disappear right after meeting with his school mates? Bit too much of a coincidence, if you ask me.'

'He'll show up if he needs dialysis,' said Lina.

'If he's still alive,' said Pat.

They didn't have to wait long. George Young's body was found two days later in a culvert, about twelve kilometres south of Peterborough, where an unsealed track signposted as Simon Road intersected with Cleary Road, the secondary road linking Peterborough to the Barrier Highway north of the tiny historic township of Terowie. Next to the body lay a twenty-two rifle, which, it appeared, George had used to kill himself by holding the barrel under his chin and reaching down to squeeze the trigger with the fingers of his right hand.

The rifle was unregistered. The mark, made by the firing pin on the cartridge to discharge the round lodged in George's skull, matched the mark on the cartridge retrieved from the bush grave in Red Banks Conservation Park that had held the remains of Jane Edwards and Andrew White for thirty years.

CHAPTER 18

PAT READ the forensic report on the scene of George Young's death. He and Lina had been released temporarily from the taskforce to explore the implications of the evidence attached to George Young's disappearance and apparent suicide.

The first thing Pat noticed in the images that formed an integral part of the report was the amount of water around the body. Unfortunately, from a forensic analysis perspective, it had rained between the time George Young had gone missing and his body had been found, thanks to the unseasonal weather pattern that had dumped a record-breaking amount of rain across the northern parts of the state. In fact, his body had been discovered by a farmer who had stopped to investigate why there was still so much water on the road the day after the rain had stopped falling.

If there had been anybody with George at the time he'd died, all traces of their presence had been erased by the water which had accumulated in the roadside channel where his body had impeded its flow through the culvert.

'Long way to walk for a bloke as sick as George,' said

Lina. 'Would take a fit person a couple of hours or more to walk that far.'

'And, he was carrying a rifle,' said Pat. He flicked through the photographs of the scene. 'No sign of a bag or strap. You'd think someone would have noticed a bloke walking along carrying a rifle in his hand.'

'You're assuming someone was using that road,' said Lina. 'Have you checked? It's in the middle of nowhere.'

'Our boy was using it,' said Pat, 'and the farmer that found the body. You got the post mortem report?'

'Yeah. It's just come through.'

'What's the time of death?'

Lina scanned through the post mortem. 'This is interesting, Pat. He's listed the cause of death as asphyxiation. The bullet wound is post mortem.'

That definitely changes things, thought Pat. 'Not suicide then?'

'Doesn't look like it,' said Lina. 'We'd better let the inspector know.'

Pat nodded. 'I'll give him a call. What's the time of death?'

'Between midday and midnight on the Friday,' said Lina.

'We know he was still alive around two that day,' said Pat. 'That's when he left the pub in Peterborough with Grant and Maitland.'

'You think they had something to do with this?'

Pat leant back in his chair. 'Let's assume the rifle belongs to Young. What does that tell us?'

Lina smiled. 'There's something wrong with their alibi for the night Edwards and White were killed.'

'If we assume the rifle belongs to either Maitland or Grant we have the same problem,' said Pat.

'It places one of them or all of them at the grave in Red Banks,' said Lina.

'We're going to need some search warrants,' said Pat. 'I'd like to search the properties of all three of them. You start on those while I brief the inspector.'

'What if the rifle belongs to someone else?' said Lina.

'Then we'll need to find out who that someone else is.'

Lina parked in the street at the address they'd been given for Julie Young. They were outside a group of six small units sitting in a rectangle of bare concrete and grass that had been lawn before the heat of summer had sucked all the life out of it.

They knocked on the door of number three and waited. There was a scraping sound and the door opened a fraction. 'What do you want?'

'We're looking for Mrs Young, Mrs Julie Young,' said Pat.

'Who are you?'

'Police,' said Pat, holding out his identification. 'I'm Detective Sergeant Travers and this is Detective Constable Palumbo.'

The door opened a little wider and Pat could see a short, white haired woman staring at his identification card. He noticed the security chain. 'Are you Mrs Julie Young?'

'Yes, I'm Julie Young.'

The door closed. They heard the sound of the security chain being disengaged and then the door opened again. They were confronted by an elderly woman, dressed in a floral housecoat, leaning on a walking stick. 'Is this about George?'

'Yes,' said Pat. 'May we come in?'

'If you must,' said Julie, turning her back and making her way slowly to the armchair next to the window, the only seat in her tiny flat that gave her a view of the world outside.

The only other chairs in the room were under the small dining table at the kitchen end of the living area. Pat pulled them out and he and Lina sat on them, a short distance from Mrs Young. Pat looked around the room. It was neat and tidy but sparsely furnished. He'd been told the units belonged to a community housing association that provided accommodation for retired single women but he hadn't expected them to be so spartan, and it appeared Julie Young had not brought many possessions with her when she'd moved in.

'We're sorry about what happened to your son,' said Pat, 'but we need to ask you a few questions.'

'What about?'

'George,' said Pat. 'When was the last time you saw him or had any contact with him?'

'Oh, I haven't seen him in years,' said Julie. 'He doesn't come to see me.'

Pat waited. Julie sat silent.

'What about phone calls?'

Julie looked at him. Pat thought he'd startled her and wondered if she was still in the room with them.

'I rang him when I heard about the funeral of those children he went to school with,' said Julie. 'I knew he wasn't well but I thought his girlfriend might take him to the funeral.'

'What did he say?' said Pat.

'Said he didn't ever want to go back to Burra,' said Julie.

'Do you know why?' said Pat.

Julie placed her hands in her lap. 'I suppose you know we used to live there?'

Pat nodded. 'We've spoken to Ross Sloane, Mrs Young. Do you remember him?'

'Yes,' said Julie. 'He was good to me. My husband wasn't a very nice man, Sergeant. He did terrible things to me and the children. Ross Sloane was good to me after what happened.'

'And, what did happen?' said Pat.

Silence. Pat thought she wasn't going to answer.

'George shot his father,' said Julie. 'It was the only way we could stop him abusing the girls.'

Pat glanced at Lina. That wasn't what he'd expected to hear.

'I thought your husband's death was treated as a suicide,' said Pat.

'We made it look that way,' said Julie, 'but what's the point of pretending now that George is dead. It's not as though you can charge him with murder, is it?'

Pat wondered how big a bucket of worms the truth about Fred Young's death would open if he did anything about it, and decided he'd think about it later when he had time to work through the implications. He brought his attention back to the current investigation.

'Someone made George's death look like a suicide,' said Pat, wondering whether that was simply ironic or someone trying to tell them something.

'Perhaps it was,' said Julie. 'I know I've found it difficult to live with knowing what I know. It must have been harder for George.'

'Your son didn't kill himself, Mrs Young.'

'That's not what your people said when they came to tell me he was dead,' said Julie.

'Yes, I know it looked that way when he was found but the autopsy results tell a different story,' said Pat. 'George was suffocated, Mrs Young, not shot as we first believed.'

'Doesn't make any difference to me, Sergeant. He's still dead.'

'Makes a difference to us, though, Mrs Young. It means somebody murdered him and then tried to make it look as though he'd killed himself.'

Julie looked down at her hands in her lap. 'You know he didn't have long to live, don't you? Only a matter of months he told me.' She looked at Pat. 'Maybe he came to some arrangement with that woman he was living with. What's her name?'

'Sylvia,' said Lina. 'Sylvia Waters.'

'Did George have access to a twenty-two rifle back in 1991?' said Pat.

'Oh, I'm sure we had one,' said Julie, 'but we sold off everything on the farm when the bank foreclosed on us. Why did you want to know that?'

'Who handled the sale?' said Pat.

'Elders,' said Julie, 'we owed them money as well.'

Pat made a note to follow up with Elders in his notebook and then looked at Mrs Young. 'The rifle found next to George was used in the murder of Jane Edwards.'

Julie fixed Pat with a stare he felt go straight through him. 'I was there when his friend picked him up that day and I can tell you he didn't have a rifle with him when he left our place. That's somebody else's gun, Sergeant. You're not pinning that on George.'

'I'm not trying to,' said Pat. 'I'm trying to find out who killed him.'

'I have no idea,' said Julie.

'Did either of your daughters keep in contact with him, Mrs Young?'

'I wouldn't know,' said Julie. 'They don't talk to me.'

'Any idea where they are?'

Julie shook her head. 'I haven't seen either of them in over twenty five years, Sergeant. George is the only one who kept in contact. They haven't forgiven me for what their father did to them.'

***

They sat in the car after leaving Julie Young's tiny flat.

'What are we going to do about that?' said Lina.

'Let sleeping dogs lie,' said Pat. 'Opening that can of worms isn't going to help us find out who killed George.'

'I guess there would have been an inquest,' said Lina.

'Probably, but I'm not challenging their findings,' said Pat. 'Sounds like he might have had a good reason for doing it, don't you think? Not sure I'd want to drag the family through that again?'

'Just as well I didn't take any notes, then,' said Lina. 'What did you make of her story about George and the twenty-two?'

Pat shrugged. 'It's not like you'd take a rifle to an end of school party, is it? But Elders might still have a record of the items sold in their archive if we're lucky.'

'Those Elders' records will be a long shot,' said Lina.

'But if that rifle did belong to George's father, we might

find out who bought it, and that might lead us to whoever used it on George.'

———

The following day they drove to Peterborough to interview Sylvia Waters.

'Tells us about the last time you saw George,' said Pat, sitting in the same chair he'd occupied the day they'd interviewed George.

'I drove him down to the pub around twelve,' said Sylvia. 'He liked to catch up with his mates and watch the horses on the big screen.'

'Did you know who he was meeting at the time?'

Sylvia shook her head. 'He didn't say. He didn't mention those fellows from Burra who reckoned they dropped him off here after lunch.'

'Were you home when they dropped him off?' said Pat.

'No, we were over at my sister's place.'

'When did you get home?'

'I tried ringing him around three when we were leaving my sister's place,' said Sylvia. 'That's when he'd usually call me to come down and pick him up. He didn't answer, so I called the pub. They told me he'd left around two with the blokes he'd had lunch with.'

'So, what time was it when you got home?'

'About half past three. My sister lives out on the road to Orroroo.'

'Any sign George had been here?'

'No. The place was still locked up,' said Sylvia. 'I tried calling him again but he didn't answer.'

'Did you speak to any of the neighbours?'

'Only Mrs Rankin in number thirteen was home. Said she heard a car stop and then leave again sometime after two, but she didn't see anything.'

Pat had read the statements the local constables had taken from the neighbours. One of them had reported seeing a white Toyota Land Cruiser turning onto Threadgold Street from Clair Street, not long after two on the Friday George Young had disappeared. The unanswered question was whether George Young had climbed out of the Land Cruiser that had transported him home from the Peterborough Hotel or been driven to his death.

'Is there any way George could have walked out to where his body was found?' said Lina.

'You saw how sick he was,' said Sylvia. 'He had trouble walking from the car into the pub.'

'Did he own a rifle?' said Pat.

'No,' said Sylvia', 'and I don't own one either, in case you want to know.'

'So, what were your movements after you got back here?' said Pat.

'I left Talia here in case he turned up and I drove down to the pub and back, and around to the hospital in case he'd had a turn. Then I went to the police station.'

Pat had seen that report as well. She'd reported him missing at ten to five.

'Then I came home and we waited.'

'I know this is going to sound callous, Ms Waters, but do you have anything to gain from George's death?'

'I wish,' said Sylvia. 'It's not like George had a fortune, Sergeant. He did say something about me getting his super-annuation when he died, but why would I kill him for it? It's not like I couldn't wait for a couple of months.'

'Yes, I've seen the autopsy report,' said Pat. 'Do you think George could have asked someone to help him stage his death as a suicide?'

'You don't think it was suicide?'

'He was suffocated before he was shot,' said Pat. 'Someone either helped him or he's been murdered.'

'Well, it wasn't me,' said Sylvia. 'I was here with Talia and there's no way I would have agreed to that.'

'Any idea who would have wanted to kill him?'

Sylvia shook her head.

'He hadn't been threatened or anything?' said Pat.

'He started having nightmares after your last visit,' said Sylvia. 'He was thrashing about in bed and talking nonsense. Said it was something from his childhood that your visit had stirred up.'

'We spoke to his mother,' said Lina. 'Sounds like George's father was violent.'

'That might explain why I couldn't get him to talk about his past. It was quite a shock finding out he'd gone to school with those kids that had been killed in Burra all those years ago.'

'Anybody else in Peterborough you think we should talk to? You know, someone who might know more about him?'

'Guess you could try Harry Williams at the Council Depot. George worked with him for years.'

As they got back into their car, Pat couldn't help noticing the similarity in the layout of this part of Peterborough with the street where Sue Marshall lived in Burra. Both streets fronted vacant land. Both streets were good locations for abducting someone, even in broad daylight.

CHAPTER 19

JOHN GRANT WAS SHIFTING SHEEP. Rotating the flock between pastures was part of the regenerative agriculture regime John had incorporated into his farm management style when he'd taken over running the property from his father. It was an approach to farming he hoped his son Jarvis would continue when he eventually took control of the place. He shut the gate and climbed back into the AG-Pro 850 he used to move around the farm, and waited for his dog to jump up onto the seat beside him.

His mobile rang. He glanced at the screen. Paul Maitland.

'Bob Davenport been to see you?' said Paul.

'Yeah. Told him we dropped George home at his place in Peterborough. He can't pin anything on us as long as we stick to our story.'

'What about the twenty-two?' said Paul.

'It's never been registered,' said John. 'My old man only registered the guns he could find when they changed the rules, and I'd made sure that one had been lost by then.'

For a moment, neither of them spoke and John wondered if that was all Paul was worried about.

'Do you think that detective bloke from Adelaide will come back?' said Paul.

John watched his sheep wander further into the paddock, away from where he sat outside the gate. 'Don't know. Bob Davenport said they were treating it as suicide. Apparently George was a lot sicker than he let on.'

'That might work in our favour,' said Paul.

'Silly bugger should have accepted our offer,' said John.

'We did the right thing,' said Paul. 'There's no knowing what he'd have done once he had that idea in his head.'

'Didn't give us much choice,' said John. 'Anyway, what's done is done. Take care.'

John ended the call and sat looking into the distance. There was none of the thrill he'd felt the night they'd killed Andrew and Jane. None of the lust that had motivated their pack rape of Jane. He shook his head, recalling the surprise he'd felt when Andrew, who he'd always thought of as a nerd without the balls to stand up to anyone, let alone the three of them, had tried to stop them. Paul had taken him down with a punch Andrew hadn't seen coming.

He could still see the look on Andrew's face before he fell back and hit his head on a rock, and lay still. They'd left him there, sprawled on the ground, and taken turns with Jane before realising he was dead. He recalled the sense of panic he'd felt the moment Jane had started screaming, and the adrenalin rush that had coursed through him when he'd shot her.

Somehow, killing George felt different. He didn't feel any sense of satisfaction. He hadn't been motivated by lust or wanting revenge. This time they'd been driven by fear. Back then, when they'd taken out Andrew and Jane, it seemed like they had nothing to lose. Now he had everything to lose. Back then, his guilt had reformed him. Now, it was gnawing at his innards. He pushed the image of George writhing on the back seat of the Land Cruiser with a plastic bag over his head to the back of his mind, and told himself to get on with his life. George had gotten what he deserved for threatening them.

Lorna Maitland walked into the offices of Owens Solicitors in Chapel Street shortly after ten on the Thursday morning after George Young's body had been discovered. Rebecca Grant was sitting at the desk in the reception area working on a document.

'Got time for a chat, Becky?'

'Sure. What's on your mind?'

Lorna smiled. 'Nothing I need a lawyer for.'

'So, this is not a billable visit, then,' said Rebecca, putting down her pen. 'Do you want to go for a coffee?'

'Think we'd better keep this somewhere private,' said Lorna. 'I'm worried.'

'Oh, about what?'

'Paul's been acting strange ever since the day he and John went to see their friend in Peterborough, you know the one they found dead last Wednesday.'

'George Young,' said Rebecca. 'That was a bit of a shock, especially after Jane and Andrew being found. We were all at school together.'

'I'd never heard of George until those bones turned up

out at Red Banks,' said Lorna, 'and then he called one day out of the blue. Wanted to talk to Paul.'

'When was that?' said Rebecca.

'The morning of the funeral.'

'I thought he'd come,' said Rebecca, 'but John says he was too sick to travel. Kidney problems or something.'

'You don't think the boys had something to do with his death, do you?'

'They were best mates at school,' said Rebecca. 'I can't imagine them doing something like that.'

Lorna wrung her hands together. 'Paul's never said much about his time at school. It's like it's something he wants to forget.'

'Well, he was a bit of a ratbag,' said Rebecca. 'So was John, to be honest. But he turned out alright in the end.'

'I guess they all grow up sometime,' said Lorna. 'I can't wait for David to get there.'

'He'll get there.'

'Has John said anything about the day they went to Peterborough?'

'Not really,' said Rebecca. 'Only about what George told them he'd been doing since they last saw him.'

'Maybe I'm worried about nothing,' said Lorna. 'Perhaps he's just upset about finding out how sick George was and then hearing that he'd killed himself.'

'That's probably it,' said Rebecca. 'Come on, let's go and have a coffee. I'll just let Dad know I'm popping out.'

———

Rebecca Grant sat in her office after having coffee with Lorna Maitland. She hadn't said anything to Lorna, but she'd been troubled by the changes in John she had noticed since they'd heard the bones found in the conservation park were the remains of Jane and Andrew. She'd put it down to the impact of finding out their friends had been killed thirty years ago. But now, after what Lorna had told her, she wasn't so sure.

Initially, she'd hoped Andrew and Jane had run off and eloped like the young lovers they'd read about but, as time passed, she'd realised that was as much a fantasy as the novels they'd enjoyed discussing in the book club. Until their remains had been found, she'd never really thought about who may have killed them or why. Now it was a constant question she asked herself, even though she thought they'd probably never know who it was.

But, after her chat with Lorna, she wondered whether John and his friends had known more about it than they'd let on. There was something about the timing of events around the death of George Young that didn't quite feel right. There was something there she wasn't sure she wanted to explore, because the answer might rock the foundations of her marriage and shatter her children's lives.

Rebecca looked at her watch. She had an appointment in thirty five minutes. She'd have to come back to her concerns some other time.

CHAPTER 20

PAT SAT in the interview room of the Burra Police Station. Across the table from him, John Grant sat next to his lawyer, a young man in a suit and tie from a law firm with offices in Clare. Pat waited for Lina to activate the video recording equipment and then stated the time and names of those present.

'I've read the statement you gave Sergeant Davenport concerning your meeting with George Young,' said Pat. 'Is there anything in that statement you wish to change, Mr Grant?'

'No,' said John.

'So, if I've understood it correctly, you and Paul Maitland met George for lunch at the Peterborough Hotel and then drove him home?'

'That's right.'

'How did George appear to you on the day?'

John glanced at his lawyer, who nodded. 'To be honest, Sergeant, he looked like shit. Kidney problems, apparently. Said he didn't have all that much time left.'

'And, what prompted that meeting?' said Pat. 'When I

spoke to you earlier, you told me you hadn't seen George for years.'

'He called Paul the morning of the funeral,' said John. 'He was too sick to come but wanted to catch up for old times sake before it was too late.'

Pat thought that sounded reasonable but wondered whether it was the truth or a constructed story. 'Did you cut across to the Barrier Highway on Cleary Road when you drove home from Peterborough?'

'Is that what the road's called?' said John.

'Did you come that way?'

'Yeah, that's the shortest way back to Burra,' said John.

'Are you aware of where Simon Road intersects with Cleary Road, Mr Grant?'

'I don't go up there very often, Sergeant. I don't know what any of the side roads are called or where this Simon Road is.'

'It's about twelve kilometres south of Peterborough along Cleary Road,' said Pat. 'Any idea how George managed to get himself that far out of Peterborough?'

'You're asking my client to speculate,' said the lawyer.

'It's only speculation if he doesn't know the answer,' said Pat.

'Are you suggesting my client knows the answer?' said the lawyer.

'I'm asking him if he does,' said Pat.

'I've got no idea,' said John. 'We left him at his house around twenty past two. If you ask me, someone must have given him a lift because there's no way he could have walked that far. He could hardly walk up his driveway when we dropped him home.'

'Are you aware a rifle was found with his body?' said Pat.

'Bob did say it looked like he'd shot himself,' said John, 'so I guess he must have used some sort of gun.'

'It was a twenty-two rifle,' said Pat. 'An old one that's never been registered.'

'Perhaps George kept one from the farm,' said John. 'Everyone around here has a twenty-two rifle, Sergeant. You can't survive on a farm without one.'

'How many do you have?'

'Four rifles and a couple of shotguns,' said John, 'but they're all registered and kept in the gun safe. Bob was out doing a registration and storage check last week. All present and accounted for I'm happy to say.'

'Well, if the rifle found next to George's body belonged to him, Mr Grant, we have a little problem,' said Pat, 'which is why I asked you to come in with your lawyer.'

The look on John's face told Pat he had no idea what Pat was talking about. 'What?' What problem?'

Pat extracted a page from the folder on the table in front of him. 'This is the list of items found in the grave at Red Banks along with the remains of Jane Edwards and Andrew White.' He pointed to where he had used a yellow high-lighter on the list. 'One of the items was a spent .22LR cartridge.' He looked at John, who didn't seem at all worried. 'That cartridge had been fired by the rifle someone wanted us to believe George Young had used to kill himself.'

John looked at his lawyer and shrugged. 'What's he saying?'

'What are you saying, exactly, Sergeant?' said the lawyer.

'If the rifle belongs to George, did he fire the round that led to this cartridge being found in the grave at Red Banks?' said Pat, tapping his finger on the sheet of paper on the table in front of them. 'And, if it was George who fired that shot,

Mr Grant, it would appear you both lied about where you were on that night in November 1991.'

John folded his arms. 'George could have picked up that rifle anywhere in the last thirty years.'

'Or maybe it never was George's rifle,' said Pat.

'What?' said John. 'Now you've got me confused.'

Pat slipped another sheet of paper out from his folder. 'This is from the post mortem report written by the patholo-gist who examined George Young's body. It lists the cause of death as asphyxiation.'

'What?' said John. 'Bob said he'd shot himself.'

'That's what someone wanted us to believe,' said Pat, 'but that's not the case according to the pathologist. It says here the most likely cause of death is asphyxiation, and there's bruising on the arms consistent with someone holding them firmly while the victim struggled to breathe.'

'That sounds horrible, but it's got nothing to do with me or Paul,' said John. 'We left him in Peterborough.'

Pat leant back in his chair to get a good look at John Grant. 'Strike you as odd at all, Mr Grant, that whoever wanted us to believe George had shot himself also wanted to let us know he'd shot Jane Edwards?'

'Who? George or someone else?'

'That depends on whose rifle it is,' said Pat. 'Not yours by any chance, is it?'

John smiled. 'Nice try, Sergeant, but as I said, all my rifles are accounted for. Check with Bob Davenport.'

'Oh, I have,' said Pat, 'and I noticed every one of them was first registered after 1996.'

'I didn't own any before then,' said John. 'Any guns on the farm before I came back from Roseworthy would have belonged to my father.'

'And what happened to them when you took over the farm?'

'Registrations were transferred to me,' said John.

'What about any guns that had never been registered prior to 1996?'

'We didn't have any after the amnesty,' said John. 'Dad either registered them or surrendered them.'

'Well it looks like someone around here didn't do that,' said Pat.

'What do you mean?' said the lawyer.

'Someone held on to the rifle used to murder Jane Edwards and used it to put a bullet into George Young's body, and that rifle has never been registered.'

'Well, unless you can prove that was my client, Sergeant, I think we're done here.'

'Thanks for coming in, Mr Grant.'

Pat terminated the interview.

Ten minutes after John Grant had left with his lawyer, Sgt Davenport ushered Paul Maitland and his lawyer into the interview room for Pat to question.

Paul stuck to the story recorded in the statement he'd given to Sgt Davenport the day George Young's body had been found and expressed a similar level of surprise to that shown by John Grant when informed George had not shot himself. When confronted with the details of the cartridge found in the grave at Red Banks, and the fact that it had been fired from the rifle found next to George's body, Paul simply shrugged and reminded Pat that Sgt Davenport had completed a registration check of the guns stored on his property on the day he'd interviewed him and found everything in order.

Half an hour later, Pat thanked Paul for coming in and let him leave.

After their interviews, Pat and Lina set out on the two hour trip back to Adelaide.

'What do you think?' said Pat, as they turned onto the Barrier Highway and headed south. 'Can we trust either of these blokes?'

'What makes you think we can't?' said Lina.

'Something just doesn't feel right,' said Pat, 'but I can't put my finger on it.'

'It's their stories,' said Lina. 'They sound rehearsed. If you read their statements they're almost word perfect.'

'That could be because they're true,' said Pat. 'Two versions of the same set of events.'

'Or a concocted story,' said Lina.

'Which one?' said Pat.

'Could be both,' said Lina. 'When I read the statements the three of them gave in 1991, I got the distinct impressions they were all reading from the same hymn sheet.'

Pat gazed out the window at the passing countryside and considered their options. They didn't have anything directly linking Grant and Maitland to Young's death. All they had was three old friends catching up after a long time following the funeral of two of their school friends, and the coincidence of George Young turning up dead twelve kilometres from home alongside the road his two friends had used to return home. Or was it more than coincidence? Trouble was he couldn't prove it was anything else.

'Whoever left that rifle with George's body obviously wasn't aware of the cartridge left behind at Red Banks.'

'Or they wanted to frame George,' said Lina.

'That would hardly be Grant and Maitland,' said Pat. 'That would blow their alibi.'

'That means there must be a third party,' said Lina, 'someone who either wanted George dead or who had agreed to help him kill himself and make it look like suicide.'

'I'm inclined to believe he was murdered,' said Pat. 'If he had the rifle, why didn't he just shoot himself? After all, if what his mother told us is true, he knew how to use a rifle. Nah, I reckon someone wanted him dead and simply wanted us to think he'd shot himself.'

'Guess they'd have gotten away with it if the body hadn't been found so soon,' said Lina. 'Pretty hard to see those little haemorrhages when there's no facial tissue.'

'We need a motive,' said Pat. 'Grant and Maitland may have had opportunity, but why would they have wanted to kill him?'

'We need the provenance of that rifle,' said Lina.

CHAPTER 21

ON THE SATURDAY morning after her husband had been interviewed by the police, Rebecca Grant was in the kitchen of their homestead eating poached eggs on toast for breakfast, when her fourteen-year-old son, Simon, joined her.

'Where's Dad?' said Simon.

'He went into town,' said Rebecca. 'You should have gotten up earlier if you wanted to go with him.'

'Is Dad in trouble?' said Simon.

'Not that I know of,' said Rebecca. 'Why do you ask?'

'The boys at school said the police are asking if anyone's missing an old twenty-two rifle.'

'Are they?'

'It was on the news.'

'Oh. I must have missed it.'

'Has Dad said anything? He listens to the news.'

'Why would he say anything about that? Sergeant Davenport checked our gun cupboard with your father when he was here. There's nothing missing.'

Simon put four Weet-Bix into a cereal bowl and covered

them with milk, before sitting down next to his mother at the table.

'Did you know there was an old twenty-two wrapped up in an oilskin under the bench at the back of the implement shed?'

Rebecca put down her coffee mug. 'What do you mean there was?'

'I found it last year,' said Simon. 'It's not there anymore. I checked when I got home from school yesterday.'

Rebecca felt a constriction in her chest. 'Did you tell your father about it?'

Simon shook his head. 'I thought it was something Grandpa had put there and forgotten about. It was old.'

'Did you touch it?'

'I only unwrapped it and wrapped it up again,' said Simon. 'I only remembered it was there when the boys said the police were asking about a missing old twenty-two.'

Rebecca thought about what that might mean and who would have known it was there. And, when it had gone missing.

'When did you find it?'

'When Dad was seeding last year. He asked me to get him the big screwdriver when he was working on the tractor. I knocked the tin of screws off the bench. I found it when I was picking up the screws.'

'Well, we will have to ask your Dad about it, won't we?'

'What if it's the one the police have?' said Simon.

'Would you recognise it?' said Rebecca, hoping he'd say no.

'It's got a circle with the letter Gee inside it on one side of the stock,' said Simon.

'Maybe your father shifted it or Grandpa remembered it was there and took it home with him.'

'When's Grandpa coming to visit?' said Simon.

'I'm not sure,' said Rebecca. 'He hasn't been feeling that well.'

'Can we go and see him?' said Simon. 'We can ask him about the rifle.'

'We'll see,' said Rebecca. 'Now finish your breakfast and go and do your chores before Dad gets home.'

Rebecca felt sick just thinking about the rifle. She didn't know what to think. Why would John or his father have hidden a twenty-two under the bench in the implement shed. She'd hardly ever been into the implement shed, and she'd never looked under the bench along its back wall.

She asked Simon to show her where he'd found the rifle. He shone his torch on the underside of the bench and showed her the wire ties that had been used to hold the wrapped weapon in place.

'It was there, Mum.'

'How did you get it down?'

'I untwisted the ties and then put it back,' said Simon. 'I didn't say anything to Dad in case I wasn't supposed to touch it.'

Rebecca thought of the times John had shouted at the boys for touching things he'd told them to leave alone and wondered how he'd react when she asked him about the rifle. 'You did the right thing, darling. Let me ask Dad about it.'

She sent Simon off to finish his chores and went back into the house and called John's father, Warren Grant.

'Pop, do you remember wrapping up a twenty-two and attaching it to the underside of the bench in the implement shed?'

'Why would I do something like that, Becky?'

'Simon says he found one there last year. An old twenty-two with a circle with a Gee inside engraved on the stock.'

There was silence for a moment.

'Is that where that got to?' said Warren. 'I thought we'd lost it. That's the twenty-two my father gave me when I left school. I looked all over the place for it when we had to register the guns after Port Arthur. Who would have put it there?'

Who indeed, thought Rebecca, suspecting she already knew the answer.

'Trouble is, Pop, it's not there anymore.'

'Anyone could have gotten into that shed,' said Warren.

'But you'd have to know the gun was there, Pop. It was wrapped up and wired to the underside of the bench. Simon only found it because he'd dropped something on the ground next to the bench.'

'He hasn't taken it, has he?'

'He's just told me about it after hearing the police are asking about anyone missing an old twenty-two.'

'Better ask John.'

'I will when he gets home,' said Rebecca.

John Grant was an only son, an only child in fact, so if anyone had hidden his father's twenty-two, he was the prime candidate in Rebecca's eyes. Maybe he'd done it in an act of revenge, to get back at his father for his harsh brand of parenting. Hiding his father's favourite gun to get back at him for some real or imagined slight was the sort of thing she could imagine John doing. She hoped that would be the explanation. But why had the rifle disappeared from its hiding place? She hoped John would have a good answer to that question. But what was she going to do if he didn't?

She called her father. Reg Owens answered on the third ring.

'Dad, I need your advice on something.'

'And what would that be on, Becky?'

'Have you been following the news on George Young's death?'

'Heard the police are treating it as murder.'

'Simon says they're asking about anyone missing an old twenty-two rifle.'

'That was on the news last night.'

Rebecca told him about the rifle Simon had found wrapped in oilcloth under the bench in the implement shed and how it had gone missing and her conversation with John's father.

'So, it's been missing since at least 1996,' said Reg.

'Possibly earlier,' said Rebecca, 'but what if it turns out to be the gun found with George's body?'

'I guess that's going to depend on how it got there, Becky.'

'What do you mean, Dad?'

'Perhaps John gave it to George when he went to see him.'

'That might make sense if George had killed himself,' said Rebecca, 'but the police are saying he was murdered.' She stopped talking, not sure she could voice the words. She took a deep breath and let them out. "What if John killed him, Dad?'

'Why would he do that?'

'What if George knew something John didn't want anybody to find out, something terrible?'

'Oh, shit!' said Reg. 'Paul Maitland was with him the day he went to see George, wasn't he?'

Rebecca heard the sound of the Land Cruiser driving into the yard. 'Got to go, Dad. John's home.'

John walked into the kitchen with the shopping bags holding the supplies Rebecca had asked him to pick up in town and the Saturday papers. John liked to spend his Saturday afternoons reading the papers.

'Simon says the police are asking if anyone's noticed if one of their twenty-twos has gone missing,' said Rebecca.

'Yeah, it's in the Advertiser on page three,' said John. 'They've got a photo.'

Rebecca took the paper from him and turned to page three. She studied the image, paying particular attention to the stock. There was no circle with a Gee inside it but there was a patch of lighter coloured wood on the side of the stock. 'Is this yours, John?' She pointed at the photograph of the twenty-two.

'All our guns are in the gun safe, sweetheart. You know that, you were here when Bob Davenport checked them.'

Something in the tone of his voice irritated her but she pressed on. 'Simon tells me there was a rifle wrapped in oilcloth hidden under the bench in the implement shed. What do you know about that?'

John leant back on the doorframe of the doorway leading out onto the veranda and smiled. 'That was Dad's favourite rifle. His father gave it to him before I was born. I lost it,' he made air quotes with his fingers, 'after he beat the shit out of me for failing year twelve.'

'You mean you hid it where he couldn't find it?'

'Yeah. You know what a mean bastard he was. He made me search the place for it when we had to register the guns after Port Arthur. I never found it, of course.'

'So, it's been hidden since the end of 1991?'

'Yeah. I suppose I should do something about it if Simon's found it.'

Rebecca felt a wave of relief flow through her. 'That would be the responsible thing to do, John. Only trouble is, Simon says it's not where he found it. He showed me the wire ties under the bench in the shed.'

John stood up. 'What? He hasn't told anybody about the rifle has he?'

'He only told me this morning.'

'Where is he? Simon!'

Simon came into the kitchen from where he had been listening to his parents in the dining room. 'Yes, Dad.'

'Want to show me where you found this rifle you told your mother about?'

Simon looked at his mother.

'It's okay,' said Rebecca.

They crossed the yard to the implement shed and Simon led them to the bench at the back of the shed. 'Under here.' Simon squatted and pointed to the wire ties.

John squatted beside him and stared at the wires. 'That's where I hid it alright.' He stood up. 'When did you find it?'

'Last year when we were seeding,' said Simon.

'Did you touch it? Move it?'

Simon looked to his mother. 'It's alright, darling.'

'I unwrapped it to see what it was,' said Simon, 'and then put it back.'

'So where is it now?' said John.

'I don't know, Dad. I came out here to see if it was still here when I got home from school on Friday. It was gone.'

'Why did you do that?'

'The boys at school said the police were asking if anybody had lost an old twenty-two, and I wanted to make sure it wasn't ours.'

'Did you tell anybody about the rifle?'

'No.'

'Are you sure, Simon? Because somebody must have known it was here.'

'I swear, Dad. I only told Mum because it was gone.'

They stood in the gloom of the shed between the header and the bench looking at each other.

'Are you sure you didn't tell your brother?'

Simon looked like he was going to cry. 'I might have. I don't remember.'

'Maybe Jarvis moved it,' said Rebecca, deciding to step in before Simon started crying.

'I guess we'd better ask him,' said John, 'otherwise we're going to have to tell the police someone has stolen it.'

'Won't you get into trouble, Dad?' said Simon.

John tussled his son's hair. 'Probably, but it will be worth it when we see Grandpa's reaction when you tell him about it.'

CHAPTER 22

On Sunday morning, Rebecca Grant woke up to an empty bed. It looked like John had not come to bed at all after she'd left him watching television the night before. She used the bathroom, pulled on her dressing gown, and made her way through the house. John wasn't in his office and he wasn't sprawled across the couch in the lounge. When she reached the kitchen, there was an envelope leaning against the wall next to the cooktop where she couldn't miss it.

Rebecca picked up the envelope. It held one piece of paper on which John had written the word: Sorry. She rushed out onto the veranda. The Land Cruiser was gone from the yard. She went back to the room John used as his office where the gun safe was located. Two of his guns were missing: a twenty-two rifle and a shotgun. She checked the ammunition cabinet hidden inside the linen press in the corridor. The stack of boxes was significantly smaller than the one she recalled seeing when Sgt Davenport had last checked on their storage compliance.

She found her mobile and called John's number. Her call went straight through to voicemail. He'd turned off his phone. She went to the shed beside the implement shed where John kept the camping equipment he used when he went hunting with Paul Maitland. His camping gear was gone.

She called Lorna Maitland.

'Is my husband at your place?'

'I was just about to call and ask you the same question,' said Lorna. 'Paul's not here and one of his guns is missing from the safe. Did John say where they were going? Paul didn't even tell me they were going hunting.'

'I don't think they've gone hunting, Lorna. I think it's much worse than that.'

'What do you mean?'

Rebecca took a deep breath. 'I think they're on the run.'

'Why?'

'George Young,' said Rebecca. 'I think they killed him.'

'What?'

'I'm going to call Bob Davenport,' said Rebecca. 'He'll know what to do.'

Sergeant Bob Davenport drove out to the Grant homestead with Constable Jenny Worth. He parked in the yard between the implement shed and the house. It was quiet. A black kelpie wandered over from its kennel to the Police Toyota and lifted its leg to mark one of the rear tyres.

Rebecca Grant appeared on the veranda of the house with her fourteen-year-old son, Simon. Bob knew the Grant's older boy, Jarvis, was at university in Adelaide.

'Simon, can you show Constable Worth where the rifle was?' said Bob. He watched the boy, followed by the dog, lead Jenny into the implement shed. He'd instructed her to photograph the place where the rifle had been hidden. 'Shall we go inside?'

'I've put the kettle on,' said Rebecca, leading Bob into her kitchen. 'Tea? Coffee?'

'Coffee will be fine,' said Bob. 'White, no sugar.' He waited while Rebecca fixed him a coffee. 'What makes you think John is involved in the murder of George Young?'

Rebecca put the mug holding his coffee on the table and picked up the note John had left her. 'This.'

'That could simply mean he's sorry for running off.'

'It's a bit more complicated than that, I'm afraid, Bob.'

Bob sipped his coffee. 'Start at the beginning.'

Simon came in with Jenny Worth.

'Coffee?' said Rebecca.

'Yes, thanks,' said Jenny. 'White, one sugar.'

'I'll make it,' said Simon.

'You were saying,' said Bob.

'John hasn't really been himself ever since we heard about Jane and Andrew,' said Rebecca, 'but I put that down to us all being at school together. I found it hard enough to deal with myself, and then there was George's death just after they'd had lunch with him in Peterborough.'

'Did you know about that lunch?' said Bob. 'I mean, did you know he was meeting with George?'

'Not until the day you told us you thought George had committed suicide.'

Bob wondered how many other things John had not told his wife. 'That's what it looked like until they did the autopsy. Then the story changed.'

Simon sat down next to Constable Worth with her mug of coffee.

'Then, Simon heard you were asking people if they'd noticed a twenty-two missing, an old one,' said Rebecca.

'Where did you hear that, Simon?' said Bob.

'One of the boys at school said he'd heard it on the news.'

'How did you know there was a gun hidden in the shed?'

'I found it last year,' said Simon.

'Do you think you'd recognise it if you saw it again?'

'It looked like the one in Saturday's paper, except it had a circle with a Gee in it on the stock.'

'Where on the stock,' said Bob, opening an image of the rifle on his mobile and showing it to Simon.

'There,' said Simon, pointing to the patch of lighter coloured wood.

That would explain why it looked as if someone had sanded something off the stock before re-oiling it, thought Bob. 'Does your brother know about this rifle, Simon?'

'Jarvis helped me wrap it back up so nobody would know we'd found it.'

'Why was that important?'

'Dad doesn't like us touching his stuff,' said Simon.

Bob smiled. 'Dads are a bit like that sometimes.' He turned to Rebecca. 'What did John say about the rifle being there for the boys to find?'

'It's his father's. John said he hid it there to get even with his father for getting angry with him when he didn't pass year twelve the first time.'

'When was that?'

'At the end of 1991,' said Rebecca. 'His father made him repeat the year so he could get into Roseworthy. We've heard the story a thousand times, haven't we, Simon?'

Simon nodded.

Bob took a sip of his coffee. 'There's something

about the rifle found with George Young's body that's not common knowledge, but it's something John and Paul were told when they were interviewed by the detectives from Adelaide. I'm afraid it's not good news, Becky.'

'I wondered about that,' said Rebecca, dreading what she was about to hear.

'There was a twenty-two shell casing in the grave at Red Banks. It was fired by the rifle found with George.'

Rebecca dropped her head into her hands and started sobbing, uncontrollably.

'Jen, make her a cup of tea with plenty of sugar. I think she's going into shock.'

'What's wrong, Mum?' Simon looked at Bob, his face filled with confusion.

'That rifle was used to murder someone in 1991,' said Bob, 'which might be the real reason your father hid it.'

'Mum's friend,' said Simon, standing and wrapping his arms around his mother.

'I'm afraid so,' said Bob, wondering if Rebecca would be okay or if he'd have to call an ambulance.

They sat with Rebecca as she emerged from the initial shock of realising John may have killed her best friend.

'I'm sorry,' said Rebecca, blowing her nose in a tissue and wiping her eyes.

'No need to apologise, Becky. It's been a bit of a shock for all of us. Do you want us to call your parents?'

'That would be good,' said Rebecca. 'Simon, get Sergeant Davenport Grandma Fiona's number.'

'Give it to Constable Worth, Simon. She'll call your grandmother.'

Bob sat with Rebecca while Jenny went into the lounge with Simon to call Fiona Owens.

'I hope they're not at Church,' said Rebecca.

'Don't worry, we'll find them.'

'Thanks, Bob.'

Bob wasn't so sure thanks were what he deserved. 'Where does John go when he goes hunting with Paul?'

Rebecca shrugged and drank more of the sweetest cup of tea she could ever remember drinking. 'Somewhere out east, towards the river. I've never been with them.'

'What about the boys? Does he ever take them hunting?'

'He's taken them camping but never hunting. He only ever goes hunting with Paul. They've been doing it forever. I think it's just an excuse to get away from everything and drink beer, to be honest. They hardly ever bring anything back to cook.'

Bob knew what that was like. He went camping with his brothers along the banks of the Murray River most years. 'What's he taken with him?'

'His usual camping equipment but I don't know what they'd have as far as supplies go, unless he'd stocked up without telling me. He did go into town yesterday but that was before we told him about Simon finding the rifle.'

'What's he got in the way of weapons?'

'A twenty-two and one of his shotguns.'

'How much ammo?'

'Several boxes, I think. Do you want to look?'

'Might be an idea,' said Bob.

He followed Rebecca up the corridor to the linen press, where he knew their ammunition cabinet was located and waited while she entered the combination and opened the cabinet. Half the boxes he'd counted only a week or so ago were gone. Shit, thought Bob. He's taken enough ammo to start a small war.

'I hopes he rethinks this,' said Bob.

They went back to the kitchen, where Bob left Rebecca and Simon with Jenny to wait for Reg and Fiona Owens to arrive.

Outside in the Toyota, he called the Duty Sergeant at Port Pirie and explained his situation.

'Send through the details, Bob, and we'll get a statewide APB out. And, Bob, no heroics. Leave that to the STAR Group boys and girls.'

Bob sent through the details of John Grant's vehicle and the weapons he had with him and then went inside to ask Rebecca for a recent photograph he could use.

'He doesn't like having his photo taken,' said Rebecca.

'I've got one of Dad in his new hat,' said Simon.

While they were driving to the Maitland homestead north of Burra, Bob called his counterpart in Clare and asked him to show the photograph of the rifle found with George Young's body to John Grant's father.

They were crossing the cattlegrid across the entrance of the driveway to the Maitland homestead when the sergeant from Clare called him back.

'Said he couldn't be sure unless he saw the rifle, Bob, but reckons it sure looks like it.'

'Okay. I'll see if I can get the detectives from Adelaide to arrange that,' said Bob. 'Thanks.'

The Maitland homestead consisted of three stone residences and several sheds grouped in a square around a large yard of packed red earth. Each of the houses was surrounded by lush gardens, thanks to a bore that tapped into the aquifer below the ground on which they stood.

Philip Maitland, Paul's older brother, stepped out of the shade on the veranda of his house and walked across the yard to where they'd parked.

'Thanks for coming, Bob. Lorna's beside herself.'

'Anyone see him leave?'

Philip shook his head. 'Dad reckons he heard Paul's Land Rover leaving around five. Didn't think anything of it at the time. I found it in one of the back paddocks that abuts the highway, about a kilometre north of here.'

'Any idea what he took with him?'

'His swag, one of the rifles, and a couple of boxes of ammo. You know, the stuff he takes when he goes hunting with John.'

'You ever go with them, Phil?'

Philip shook his head. 'Nah, I'm not into shooting things for pleasure.'

'Any idea where they usually go?'

Philip shrugged. 'Anywhere between here and Broken Hill or out to the river. They could be anywhere.'

'It's worse than I thought,' said Bob. 'It's looking like they might have killed those kids found out at Red Banks as well as George Young. I'm sorry.'

'Bloody hell. Dad's not going to want to hear that. How's Becky holding up?'

'She's a bit of a mess,' said Bob. 'Her parents are with her. Where's Lorna?'

'I don't think she's in any fit state to talk to you, Bob.'

'I need a recent photo of Paul.'

Philip pulled his mobile phone out of his pocket and opened the photo app. He scrolled through the images. "This do?' He showed the photograph he'd taken of his brother a couple of weeks ago to Bob.

'That will do. Can you send it to me?' Bob gave him his mobile phone number.

Bob remembered Paul and Lorna had two teenage sons. 'Where are Paul's boys? He didn't take them with him by any chance, did he?'

'They're at school in Adelaide,' said Philip.

'You better get news to them before this hits the airwaves.'

'We've called the school. Mum's on her way down to pick them up.'

Bob wondered what they'd said to the school but realised, in the greater scheme of things, it didn't matter.

'Let me know if he makes contact with any of you, Phil.'

'Will do.'

Bob watched Philip walk towards the house, climb the steps up to the veranda, and disappear into the shadows he'd walked out of when they arrived.

'We better get back to the station, Jen. People are going to be looking for us.'

CHAPTER 23

PAT TRAVERS SURFACED from a deep sleep, called back into consciousness by the sound of his mobile phone ringing. He'd spent a lonely Saturday night feeling sorry for himself, watching television, and drinking more shiraz than he had intended. His head hurt. His mouth tasted like sandpaper. He closed his eyes and let the phone ring out in an attempt to return to the oblivion of sleep.

A few moments later he heard a beep. Someone had left him a message. On a Sunday morning, he assumed it was still morning, that meant it could only be work.

He reached across to the bedside table, picked up the phone and pressed the home button. The screen lit up. It was ten twenty six. Time he was out of bed, even if he had the weekend off. He checked the recent calls list. The missed call was from DI Smith.

Pat got out of bed and used the bathroom. He rinsed his mouth with water from the tap over the washbasin and looked at his bloodshot eyes in the mirror. He had to stop doing this to himself.

He listened to the message the inspector had left and did as he was asked.

'Morning, sir,' said Pat, when DI Smith answered.

'Pat, those blokes you interviewed in Burra last week have gone to ground and taken their guns with them. STAR Group have been called in to help with the search but I want you up there to work with the locals.'

So much for Sunday at home, thought Pat. 'Right, sir.'

'Take Palumbo with you, Pat. Seeing the STAR Group in action will be a good experience for her.'

'Yes, sir.'

Pat ended the call and sat on the side of the bed. It had been a while since he'd worked with officers from the Special Tasks And Rescue Group. They would take control of the situation and keep people like him away from the action and decision making, which was probably just as well since he didn't fancy running around with a gun and getting himself shot at.

He stood and looked at himself in the mirror of what had been his wife's dressing table. He needed a shower and a shave, and something to eat. It would take him a good hour to get himself ready to leave.

He called Lina, explained their situation, and arranged to meet her in Angus Street at noon.

It was two fifteen in the afternoon when they reached Burra. On the drive up, Pat had called the Burra Motor Inn and booked them in for the week. He had no idea how long they'd be in town or how much competition there would be for beds.

Lina turned into Chapel Street and parked across from the Police Station. The STAR Group's vehicles and their mobile command centre took up most of the space in the car park and the street in front of the station. Officers were climbing out of vehicles and checking equipment.

'Looks like they haven't been here long,' said Pat. 'Let's go and find out who's in charge.'

They crossed Chapel Street and entered the station. It was quiet. All the action appeared to be outside in the yard.

'Sergeant Davenport here someplace?' said Pat.

Jenny Worth looked up from her computer screen. 'He's in the briefing room with Inspector Yardley waiting for Jarvis Grant.'

'Jarvis?' said Pat.

'John Grant's older boy. Apparently he knows where his father goes camping.'

They went through to the briefing room. Bob Davenport was sitting at the table with two officers clad in black, who looked up when they entered the room.

'Ah, Inspector, this is Detective Sergeant Pat Travers,' said Bob. 'He's leading the Edwards and White investigation.'

'Inspector Yardley,' said the man, seated nearest to Bob. 'This is my 2IC, Sergeant Moss.'

'Sir,' said Pat. 'This is Detective Constable Palumbo.'

Inspector Yardley nodded at Lina. 'And, why are you here, Detective Sergeant?'

The tone of the question didn't surprise Pat. 'Because my inspector wants me here, sir.'

Inspector Yardley smiled. 'He thinks you can help, does he?'

Pat pulled out a chair for Lina and one for himself, and

then sat at the table. 'He wants to remind you we want to talk to Grant and Maitland when you find them, sir.' Pat smiled.

'This is my operation, Detective Sergeant, and my people won't need any help from you, so keep out of our way.'

'This part is your show, Inspector. We're here to pick up the pieces when you're through, but if you need any help talking to the locals, well that's our specialty.' Pat smiled. 'You only have to ask.'

'Well, perhaps you'd better sit in on our chat with young Grant when he gets here, Detective Sergeant.'

'No problems, sir,' said Pat, feeling the tension in the room fade to a more relaxed level.

'What do we know about these two fugitives?' said Sergeant Moss.

They listened as Pat went through the background information they had accumulated on Grant and Maitland.

'What makes you think they're your killers, Detective Sergeant?' said Inspector Yardley.

'The rifle found with George Young's body was used to detonate the cartridge found in the grave at Red Banks, and it's been identified by Grant's son as the one he'd seen hidden in a shed on their property.'

'How do we know that?' said Inspector Yardley.

'Grant's wife told us,' said Bob. 'He'd spun them a story about hiding it to upset his father years ago, before the gun amnesty back in the nineties, and said he'd let me know about it after they'd seen our appeal in yesterday's paper.' Bod shook his head. 'Didn't happen. He took off instead.'

Jarvis Grant arrived with his grandfather, Warren Grant. A younger and older version of John, thought Pat.

'Where do you think your father would go?' said Bob Davenport.

'Pine Creek,' said Jarvis. 'There's an abandoned homestead there. It's Dad's favourite camping spot.'

'Ketchowla Homestead,' said Bob. 'There's definitely no-one living out there and it's surrounded by hundreds of square kilometres of emptiness.'

'That's why Dad likes it there,' said Jarvis. 'Feels like you're the only people on the planet when you camp there.'

'Where else would they go?' said Pat. 'I reckon your father might suspect we'd ask you about where he'd go.'

Jarvis shrugged and looked at his grandfather.

'Anywhere they could shoot something to eat,' said Warren. 'I know they've been as far south as the river hunting feral pigs but, with all this rain, there'll be kangaroos everywhere. They could be anywhere.'

'Let's take a look at this Pine Creek,' said Inspector Yardley. 'Where is it?'

'East of Mount Bryan,' said Bob. 'Take us about an hour and a half to get there.'

CHAPTER 24

JOHN PULLED off the highway where it met Belcunda Road north of Burra and shut off the engine. In the predawn darkness, he settled in to wait for Paul. Within minutes, the lights of Paul's Land Rover appeared on the other side of the fence. He climbed out to help Paul transfer his camping equipment and supplies into the back of the Land Cruiser.

'Morning,' said Paul, as he handed his swag across the fence to John. 'I hope we're doing the right thing.'

'You want to spend the next twenty five years in Yatala?'

'Not particularly.'

They worked in silence to stow Paul's gear and then climbed into the Land Cruiser. 'Where are we going?' said Paul, closing the door.

'Bush,' said John, 'and make sure you turn your mobile off. They can use those bloody things to track us.'

Paul pulled his mobile from his pocket and switched it off. 'Not much coverage once you get off the highway out here in any case.'

'Better to be safe than sorry,' said John, starting the engine and easing the Land Cruiser back onto the highway.

'How long do you think we'll have before anyone notices we're gone?' said Paul. 'Lorna won't wake up for a couple of hours. What about Becky?'

'Probably the same,' said John.

'What have you got in the way of food?' said Paul. 'I could only put my hands on a bag of spuds, half a dozen cans of baked beans, and some cartons of long-life milk.'

'I've loaded my emergency stores, so we should have enough of the basics to hold out for a couple of weeks,' said John, 'but we can live off the land until things die down. Then we'll have to find a way to replenish our supplies. Anyway, there's plenty of game around.'

'I've got my knives,' said Paul. 'Thought we might need them. We're going to need access to water, though.'

'Be plenty of dams with water in them after the rain we've had,' said John. 'Thought we could camp at Pine Creek, away from the homestead, though. Don't want some tourist taking photos of us, do we?'

'The boys know about Pine Creek, John. We've taken them camping there often enough. We need to go somewhere nobody's going to think to look, somewhere abandoned, off the beaten track.'

John thought about the places they'd camped at on their hunting trips. 'Remember that place on Deep Creek Road out from Terowie we stayed a couple of years back?'

'The one with the cypress pines and the windmill?'

'Yeah, no-one will think to look for us there.'

'Hope the windmill's still working. That'll solve one of our problems,' said Paul.

John depressed the clutch and changed gears as the Land Cruiser picked up speed. 'At this rate, we'll be there before anyone starts looking for us.'

Shortly after sunrise, John turned the Land Cruiser off Deep Creek Road and drove over the cattlegrid across the entrance of a driveway marked by faded gateposts that had once been painted white. They followed an overgrown track for a little over a kilometre, before it crossed a dry creek bed on a concrete causeway and veered left into a grove of cypress pines enclosing a stone homestead and shearing shed, several smaller buildings, and a windmill next to a concrete tank.

Although the property had been abandoned during the drought of the early years of the century, the buildings still offered protection from the elements, their sturdiness a silent testimony to the skills of the people who had built them.

John stopped and then reversed the Land Cruiser into the loading bay of the shearing shed, where it would be difficult, if not impossible, to see from the air.

'You stay with the vehicle,' said Paul, sliding his rifle out from under his swag on the back seat. 'I'll take a look around and make sure we're alone.'

'I'll check the shed,' said John, picking up his rifle, 'while you look around outside.'

'Okay.'

John waited until Paul had crossed the yard and then walked through the interior of the shearing shed and attached shearers' quarters looking for signs of occupation. It was as they had left it on their last visit. He turned on the cold water tap in the bathroom of the shearers' quarters. Rust stained and then cool, clear water flowed into the washbasin. He flushed the toilet and heard the sound of water flowing in to refill the cistern.

While waiting for Paul to return, John found the ladder

he'd left leaning against the inside wall of the shed on their last visit and carried it out to the concrete tank that collected rainwater from the gutters of the shearing shed. He climbed the ladder and opened the lid on top of the tank. They wouldn't have to worry about operating the windmill. The tank was full and, as far as he could tell, free of contamination from floating dead birds and rodents. He secured the lid and descended the ladder, before returning the ladder to where he'd found it.

About thirty minutes after he'd left, Paul returned. 'Looks like no-one's been here since we were here last.'

'Tank's full,' said John. 'Water's running in the shearers' quarters. Let's set up in there.'

'You start on that. I'll find something to wipe out our tyre tracks from the yard.'

'You think they'll come looking here?' said John.

'They've got a bloody helicopter,' said Paul. 'We don't want to leave them any signs they can see from the air.'

John hauled out the portable generator he'd packed and carried it to the veranda attached to the kitchen of the shearers' quarters. They'd be able to boil water and cook without having to light a fire for as long as the generator's fuel supply lasted. He'd packed a fifty litre can of the stuff and hoped it would be enough. He had no idea how long the police would keep looking for them and, unless they moved to higher ground to listen to the radio, no way of knowing what was going on in the world.

An hour after arriving, they sat down to a breakfast of baked beans on toast with coffee.

'Never thought we'd end up like this,' said Paul.

'Too bad we couldn't talk any sense into George,' said John, cutting up his toast.

'What made you choose that rifle?' said Paul.

'It was the only unregistered gun I had,' said John. 'Besides, how was I to know we'd buried that cartridge with them?'

'Well, even that would have helped point the finger at George.'

'Yeah, too bad Simon hadn't told me about finding it,' said John. 'That's what's really put us in it.'

'How long do you think we'll need to stay here?'

John stirred his coffee. 'I dunno. Maybe a month. Then we can go north and reinvent ourselves.'

'What, like that bloke from Victoria that's just been found in far north Queensland after being on the run for twelve years?'

'Got any better ideas?'

'Not at the moment.'

CHAPTER 25

Bob Davenport stopped his Police Toyota about five hundred metres south of the group of buildings that had once been the heart of Ketchowla Station and studied them through his binoculars. There was no sign of movement.

The STAR Group team's black SUV that had followed him at a distance came to a halt behind the Toyota. Bob walked back to their vehicle and pointed towards the buildings visible on the open ground ahead of them.

'See anything?' said Sgt Moss, climbing out of the SUV.

'No sign of a vehicle or any movement,' said Bob, 'but that doesn't mean they're not here.'

'Right boys, let's get the bird in the sky,' said Sgt Moss.

Bob watched as the three members of the team assembled and then deployed their surveillance drone, which was equipped with both visual and thermal cameras.

The drone operator, sitting in the shade in the rear of the SUV, studied the screen of the laptop that displayed the data feed from the cameras on the drone as it swept over and around the group of buildings in front of them.

'All clear, Sarge. No sign of life.'

'Stay with your vehicle, Bob. We'll do a sweep of the area,' said Sgt Moss.

Bob watched as the squad put on their body armour and helmets, readied their weapons, and then approached the homestead behind their vehicle, before disappearing inside to clear each building.

It was all over in fifteen minutes and Sgt Moss called Bob over the radio to let him know it was all clear. Bob put the Toyota in gear and drove up to the ruins of the homestead.

'How big's this property?' said Sgt Moss, as Bob joined him.

'Around six hundred square kilometres with plenty of places to camp if you have the right equipment.'

Sgt Moss directed the drone operator to send the drone up for a bird's eye view of the surrounding terrain, while the other members of his team searched the area around the buildings for vehicle tracks.

After an hour of flight time, without detecting any sign of their fugitives or their vehicle, the operator brought the drone in to land and they returned to Burra.

Eight thirty Monday morning, the three sergeants met with Inspector Yardley in the briefing room of the Police Station.

'There have been no reported sightings of their vehicle,' said Sgt Moss.

'What's the range on the vehicle they're driving?' said Inspector Yardley.

'Three fifty to four hundred ks,' said Bob. 'Enough to get

them to Broken Hill, Mildura, half way to Mount Gambier or over to Eyre Peninsula.'

'So, they really could be anywhere by now?' said Inspector Yardley.

'There's a lot of traffic on some of those roads, sir, and we've got people looking out for them interstate as well as here,' said Bob. 'I'm inclined to think they've gone to ground around here someplace, where they know the country.'

'Makes sense,' said Inspector Yardley. 'Where do you suggest we concentrate our efforts?'

'I know there's a lot of country out there,' said Pat, 'but how many abandoned homesteads are there? Or decent places to camp?'

'Most of the decent places to camp are in national parks,' said Bob, 'but there aren't that many abandoned places where the buildings are more than ruins.'

'Can we mark them on a map?' said Inspector Yardley.

'We'll need to talk to council and Primary Industries,' said Bob. 'A lot of the properties out here are pastoral leases.'

'Okay, I'll make some calls,' said Inspector Yardley.

'What are we going to say to the media, sir?' said Sgt Moss. 'There's a gaggle of them outside.'

'Tell them I'll do a doorstop at nine-thirty, now let's see how many of these places we can uncover.'

At nine-thirty, Pat stood next to Bob Davenport in the driveway of the Police Station listening as Inspector Yardley reminded the public they were searching for two armed and dangerous fugitives.

'If you see them, do not approach them. Call Crime

Stoppers. I'm especially appealing to anyone who lives within a three hundred kilometre radius of Burra to keep your eyes open around abandoned buildings, and to contact Crime Stoppers if you notice signs of recent use of any property you know has been unoccupied for some time. Thank you.'

Inspector Yardley walked away from the microphones and back into the Police Station. The reporters looked at Pat and Bob.

'Sorry,' said Pat. 'We're not doing questions today.'

CHAPTER 26

Rebecca Grant sat at the kitchen table in the Grant homestead with her sons, empty breakfast dishes on the table between them. None of them looked as if they'd had a good night's sleep.

'What are we going to do, Mum?' said Jarvis, placing his empty coffee mug on the table in front of him.

'Wait, I suppose,' said Rebecca.

'About the farm?' said Jarvis. 'Someone has to manage the sheep and I don't think Grandpa's up to it.'

Rebecca roused herself. 'I guess you'll have to do it until your father comes home.'

'That could be a long time, if ever,' said Jarvis, 'if he's done what the police are saying he did.'

Rebecca stared at her older son. 'You think your father is a murderer?'

Jarvis glanced across the table at his brother, who shrugged. They'd spent half the night talking about it. He turned back and faced his mother. 'He's on the run, Mum. What do you think?'

Rebecca wrapped her arms around herself and looked at

the table. She couldn't bring herself to face Jarvis. It was hard enough, facing the truth. 'I don't know what to think, to be honest. Jane and Andrew were my friends. We were all friends.'

'I think we need to allow for the possibility it might be true,' said Jarvis, 'until we find out otherwise.'

Rebecca looked at Jarvis. He sounded so grown up. She knew he was right, though. Everything pointed to John being involved in the deaths of her friends, even if she didn't want to believe it.

Her whole life since she'd come back to Burra and married John now felt as if it had been a sham. She didn't know if she'd be able to stay once the truth was out or if, in fact, she'd want to. Everything in the house spoke of John. She wondered if they'd all be better off if they sold the farm and started again, somewhere else. But, it wasn't her decision to make, was it? The boys had grown up on the property. It was their home and all they'd ever talked about was being farmers, like their father.

'Grandpa said he'd come out around lunch time,' said Jarvis, ' and help me work out what needs to be done.'

'What about school?' said Simon.

'Maybe tomorrow,' said Rebecca. 'We won't be able to stay here in hiding forever.'

'I better let uni know I won't be back,' said Jarvis.

'Wait until we know what's going on,' said Rebecca.

'I can't wait forever, Mum. I need to let them know I'm withdrawing from my subjects soon, otherwise they'll fail me.'

'Can't you do it online like last year?'

'I'll need to check that out but, if I'm running the farm, I'll have to go part-time.'

Rebecca started packing up the dirty breakfast dishes. 'Look into it. There's no need to rush, is there?'

'I suppose not,' said Jarvis. 'Come on, Simon, let's go and feed the chooks. They'll be starting to wonder where we are.'

As Rebecca was putting the breakfast dishes into the dishwasher, the house phone rang. She wiped her hands and lifted the receiver from the wall-mounted handset.

'Becky, Sue Marshall. I was just talking to your mother. Are you alright?'

Rebecca leant against the kitchen bench. She hadn't expected a call from Jane's mother.

'Not really, Sue.'

'I know, it must be dreadful. How are the boys?'

'They're putting on a brave face, Sue. I don't know if they realise what it all means.'

'It's a shock to all of us, Becky. I just wanted you to know I'm here for you if you need someone to talk to, a shoulder to cry on.'

'Thanks, Sue.'

'Give me a call, anytime.'

Rebecca sat at the table with her head in her hands. She recalled the hours she'd spent with Sue in the weeks after Jane had disappeared, and her visit to console her when Jane's remains had been found.

She didn't think she'd ever be able to forgive John for what he'd done, and the more she thought about it, the more she was convinced he'd killed her friends and destroyed her life. How had he lived with himself, all these years? How many lies had he told her? Who the hell was he?

She felt herself slipping over the edge into an unfathomable abyss of despair, the darkness calling to her, promising to comfort her in her misery. She shook herself awake. She couldn't afford to allow despair to embrace her, not while she had the boys to think about. She stood up. She knew the secret was to keep busy. That had always worked for her before.

CHAPTER 27

JOHN AWOKE WITH A START. It took him a few moments to realise where he was. He looked across the room to where Paul's swag lay on the floor. It was empty. He assumed he'd find Paul making breakfast in the kitchen.

He rolled out of his swag, leaving it open to air, and made his way to the bathroom, before ambling down the corridor to the kitchen at the rear of the shearers' quarters. There was no sign of Paul. He went back into the room they were using as their campsite. Paul's rifle was gone.

He told himself Paul had probably gone out to have a look around, since they'd decided to lay low for a few days before risking using their rifles to bring down a kangaroo. Grabbing his twenty-two, he went for a walk around the shearing shed.

The Land Cruiser was still parked in the loading bay. In the early morning light, he looked out across the yard towards the homestead. Something moved, ever so slightly, in the shadows under the veranda on the western side of the house. He stood still and waited, expecting someone to bark out an order telling him to drop his weapon and come out with his hands on his head. Nothing happened. No voice called out in challenge.

Perhaps it's a kangaroo, thought John. The trees next to the house swayed in the morning breeze. The shape moved again. On closer inspection, it didn't look like a kangaroo. He lifted his rifle and sighted on the shape using the telescopic sight. The shape swaying in the shadows was Paul's lifeless body.

John lowered the rifle and hung his head. The choice his friend had made meant he was now on his own. He certainly hadn't seen Paul's decision coming, given the conversations they'd had about where they could go and what they could do to reinvent themselves once the police search died down.

He rested his rifle against the side of the loading bay and retraced his steps back to the Land Cruiser. He opened the rear door and searched through their gear until he found Paul's hunting knives. Then he walked across the yard to the homestead, stood on the box Paul had used to launch himself into oblivion, and cut the rope holding Paul's body off the floor of the veranda. The body dropped onto the wooden floorboards with a thud. The swarm of flies around the head of the body dispersed and reformed. The processes of death and decay waited for no-one.

'Christ, Paul! Why didn't you say something?'

John knew he couldn't leave the body where it was, especially if he was going to stay at the homestead until the police had scaled back their efforts to find him. He went in search of the tools he'd need to dig a grave.

Fortunately, the owners of Waterdown Station had simply walked off the property, leaving their implements behind. He found what he was looking for in the tool shed that had serviced the homestead's gardens and selected a spot in what had been the vegetable garden, where he assumed it would be easier to dig a hole in the dry earth than in the front yard next to where Paul had chosen to end his life.

Before he started digging, John crossed over to the shearers' quarters and returned with the water bag, which he'd filled at the rainwater tank and hung on the veranda outside the kitchen after they'd eaten the previous evening. The sun was already heating the day and he knew, from his long experience working on the land, that digging holes was thirsty business.

The ground was dry, despite the rain they'd received earlier in the season, and it took him close to two hours to create a suitable hole. When he was satisfied with the depth of the grave, John walked around to the western side of the house, grabbed Paul's body under the armpits, and dragged it around to the rear of the house.

He lay the body next to the hole he'd dug and stood up, stretching his back. 'Shit, Maitland. You weigh a bloody ton!'

He took another swig from the water bag, returned it to the hook under the pepper tree that shaded the kitchen windows of the homestead, and then squatted next to Paul's body.

'Too late for prayers, mate.'

John rolled the body over the edge of the hole and let it fall. Without checking to see how it had landed, he picked up the spade he'd used to dig the hole and started shovelling the dirt he'd piled up next to it back to where it had come from.

It took John a lot less time to fill in the hole than it had taken him to create it, and when he'd finished, he crossed over the yard with his water bag in search of something to eat. He was famished.

John sat on the corner of the veranda at the rear of the shearers' quarters with his back resting against the post supporting the roof. On the floorboards beside him there was a mug of coffee, that had gone cold, and behind him, leaning against the wall, his rifle. His attention was drawn to the line of little red monsters, bull ants, coming and going from a hole under one of the flagstones that separated the shearers' quarters from the stockyards attached to the shearing shed. He knew they could inflict a painful bite and reminded himself not to leave any food scraps around that might attract them into the building.

His thoughts returned to Paul. He hadn't expected his friend's final act. He'd never thought of Paul as someone who would take the easy way out, and wondered if thinking about it that way was anywhere near the truth. What if running was the easy way out?

John shook his head. That didn't make sense. He'd known Paul all his life. Their parents had been friends. They'd played together, started school together. And, they'd done some pretty stupid things together. Most of which had been harmless, until the night they decided Andrew White was not going to stop them from having their way with Jane Edwards.

That night, which he now regretted, had only happened because his parents had left him home in charge of the farm when they'd gone to Adelaide with his grandparents to attend a concert. They'd even agreed to Paul staying over to keep him company. They hadn't known about George and hadn't objected when they found out he'd joined them. Everyone in the district had felt sorry for Fred Young's kids.

It had seemed like a good idea when George had first mentioned it. They'd even drawn straws to work out the order in which they'd get their turn fucking Jane. John had drawn the winning straw, and George, ever the loser, had found himself at the end of the line, although he hadn't seemed at all concerned. In fact, he'd laughed, claiming he'd get the best fuck. And maybe he had. John hadn't enjoyed it as much as he'd anticipated. Jane had resisted and he'd had to force himself into her. The only satisfaction had come from finally having her after she'd refused him.

George, on the other hand, had been ecstatic. Jane had let him have his way with her. She'd lost all her fight after being raped twice and seeing what they'd done to Andrew. Bloody Andrew White, thought John. If he'd just done what he'd been told. But that wasn't how it had worked out. Andrew, the nerd they'd all seen as a weakling, had fought back, like a madman, when he'd realised what they intended doing to Jane.

He'd gone down like a sack of bricks when Paul had hit him, banging his head on a rock. They thought they'd knocked him out. It was only after they'd had their fun with Jane that they'd realised he was dead.

They'd stood around in dumb silence watching Jane pull her clothes back on, until John realised she wasn't going to keep her mouth shut. That when they'd loaded Andrew's body into the back of the car and taken her out to Red Banks, and drawn straws again as they'd taken turns digging the hole. John had drawn the short straw. He'd forced Jane to kneel next to the grave and look away from him, and shot her in the head with his father's twenty-two. One shot. She'd fallen into the grave on top of Andrew. They'd covered them up and gone home, and worked out their story, the story they'd stuck to for thirty years, until George had wanted to extort money from them.

John looked at his hands. They were calloused. They'd done a lot of work. He'd buried three of his friends and helped Paul kill George.

He had no recollection of ejecting the spent cartridge. It must have been an automatic action, and that action had led to their undoing. He thought he'd been clever planting the unregistered rifle on George but knew now it had been a mistake, especially after Simon had found the rifle and told his mother.

That thought made him think of Becky. He knew he hadn't deserved her but she'd loved him, at least she'd loved the person he had presented to her. She'd given him a reason to believe in himself, to redeem himself. She'd helped him make a success of the farm, with her attention to detail and willingness to earn an off-farm income in those years when the farm income hadn't been enough to pay the bills. And, together they'd brought two boys into the world: Jarvis and Simon. Two young men he was immensely proud of. He wondered what they thought of him now. He knew Rebecca would never forgive him, which was why he wasn't going home.

Maybe that's why Paul had killed himself. He couldn't face the shame of telling his family the truth or live with knowing they knew what he'd done.

John had no intention of either killing himself or facing his family with the truth. As soon as he thought it was safe to move, his plan was to head off into the great beyond and disappear forever.

He stood, intending to patrol the perimeter of his domain. As he reached for his rifle, a change in the background noise caught his attention. It sounded like a swarm of bees somewhere in the distance, but it was too late in the season for bees to be swarming.

He scanned the sky above him. He couldn't see anything. The sound receded and disappeared within the soundscape of his surroundings. John wondered if he'd imagined it or if it had been the sound of the police helicopter in the distance, looking for him in the wrong place.

He decided he'd better stay indoors, out of sight, just in case they came his way.

CHAPTER 28

Bob Davenport was in the briefing room, marking the location of abandoned homesteads on the map they'd mounted on the wall, when his mobile phone rang. He didn't recognise the number.

'Sergeant Davenport.'

'Are you that policeman in Burra?'

Bob didn't recognise the voice. 'Yes. Who am I speaking to?'

'Oh, sorry. Jim Paterson. Got your number from the bloke at the Terowie roadhouse. I manage White Stones Station.'

'Where's that?' said Bob.

'About thirty kilometres east of here, off Deep Creek Road.'

Bob located Terowie on his map and traced his finger along Deep Creek Road. 'Is that anywhere near Waterdown Station, Jim?

'That's why I'm calling,' said Jim. 'Heard you blokes on the radio this morning. Look, it might be nothing, but I reckon someone's driven up the drive into Waterdown Station, and no-one's lived there for years.'

'Recently?' said Bob.

'I'd say so,' said Jim. 'You can still see where they drove through the grass.'

'Did you stop and have a look?' said Bob.

'Yeah. I had a look, Sergeant, but I didn't go exploring. I heard what you said about these whackos being armed and dangerous. What I can tell you, though, is whoever went up that drive hasn't come back out. There's only one set of tracks.'

'Thanks, Jim. We'll take a look.'

After ending the call, Bob called Inspector Yardley, who was ensconced in his mobile command centre, to pass on the information he'd received.

'How far is that from here, Sergeant?'

'About eighty ks, Inspector.'

'Okay, I'll get a team up there to check it out.'

It was late afternoon when Bob and Pat, travelling in Bob's Police Toyota with its prisoner holding unit behind the passenger cabin, arrived at the entrance of the driveway into Waterdown Station behind the black SUV carrying the second STAR Group team. Bob watched in the rear-view mirror as the Burra ambulance rolled to a stop about twenty metres behind them.

The initial search team led by Sgt Moss, had deployed its surveillance drone to locate and examine the homestead buildings, which were out of sight in a gully about a kilo-metre away from where they stood at the entrance to the driveway. The team had confirmed John Grant's Land Cruiser was parked inside the loading bay of the shearing shed near the homestead and that at least one person was inside a smaller building attached to the shearing shed.

The STAR Group officers assembled between their vehicles and put on their body armour. Then they readied their weapons and waited. Sgt Moss deployed the drone again so he could monitor the situation in real time and keep his officers informed of their target's movements as they approached the buildings. Once the drone was airborne and the operator had confirmed the location of their target by his heat signature, Sgt Moss gave the order to proceed.

The STAR Group officers piled into their vehicles, which moved slowly up the driveway and disappeared into the gully. Bob and Pat, followed by the ambulance, drove in as far as the creek that the driveway crossed about five hundred metres before it reached the homestead, and waited.

From where they were parked, Bob could see one of the STAR Group's black vehicles. The other one had disappeared into the cypress pines surrounding the homestead buildings. He looked at the rocky landscape with its stunted trees and red dirt and wondered why on earth anyone would have believed they could make a living in such a dry and desolate place.

'Which one of them do you think it is?' said Pat.

'Dunno,' said Bob, 'but I hope he has the brains to surrender.'

CHAPTER 29

JOHN GLANCED AT HIS WATCH. It would be dark in a little over an hour. Time to think about what he was going to eat.

He went into the kitchen and rustled through his stores, looking for something to heat up for his evening meal. He was distracted from his search by the same swarming sound he'd heard earlier. He stopped and listened. It seemed to be getting louder. It wasn't loud enough to be a helicopter but, whatever it was, it definitely wasn't natural.

He stopped thinking about eating and grabbed his rifle, making sure there was a round in the chamber. Then he slipped a couple of loaded magazines into his pocket and went to investigate.

The sound seemed to be coming from the direction of the house. He made his way along the edge of the loading bay to the front of the shearing shed and stopped to listen. Without breaking cover, he looked across the yard to the homestead.

Something was moving just above the tree line. It was too big to be a bird. Within a microsecond of spotting it, he realised it was the source of the noise he could hear. He lifted his rifle to examine it through his telescopic sight but, before he could align his sight on the object, he heard the sound of a vehicle approaching at speed from the direction of the creek. He turned, just in time to see a fast moving black SUV enter the yard and stop about twenty metres from where he stood.

The doors of the SUV swung open and several black clad figures holding weapons sprung out of the vehicle and took cover behind it.

Fuck! The police. John swung his rifle around from the house to the vehicle and fired. His round bounced off the armour-plated side of the vehicle.

'Police! Drop your weapon!'

John fired again. A flash erupted from a muzzle pointed at him through the gap between an open door and the body of the vehicle. Something punched into his right shoulder and pushed him backwards. He dropped his rifle as he landed on his backside. His shoulder hurt like hell. Then he felt a boot on his chest, holding him down.

'Don't move!'

John opened his eyes and stared into the black face mask of his captor. A second officer appeared beside the first and knelt down on one knee beside him.

'Stay still, mate,' said the officer, applying a field dressing to staunch the flow of blood from John's shoulder wound. 'Ambulance is on its way.'

John closed his eyes. Fuck! The worst possible thing had happened to him. He'd been shot but he wasn't dead.

'Stay with me, mate.'

John felt his hand being squeezed and opened his eyes.

'John Grant?' said the officer.

'Yeah.'

'Where's your mate, Paul Maitland?'

John closed his eyes. He was having trouble staying focused. He felt another pair of hands on the side of his neck. He opened his eyes. There was a man in a different uniform holding a syringe.

'Just going to give you a shot of morphine, John.'

John recognised the voice but couldn't place the face, and then the world went dark.

The paramedics were loading John into the ambulance when Bob and Pat arrived outside the shearing shed. Sgt Moss was directing his officers to conduct a sweep of the area for any sign of Paul Maitland, although he knew from the drone's data feed there was no-one else at the homestead.

'Sarge,' called the drone operator, 'looks like someone's buried something in the yard behind the house.'

Bob walked along the gravel path that ran the length of the veranda towards the rear of the homestead with Sgt Moss and one of his officers.

'Sarge,' said the officer, pointing at a short length of rope swinging in the breeze from one of the veranda's rafters. 'That hasn't been there long.'

Bob looked at the rope and the ground below it. 'Someone or something's been dragged along this path.'

They examined the line of marks in the gravel stretching out ahead of them. 'Think you're right, Bob,' said Sgt Moss. 'Let's see where the trail takes us.'

They stepped off the path into the garden bed alongside it and followed the marks in the gravel around the side of the house to a mound of recently disturbed earth, in what had once been the homestead's vegetable garden.

'Looks big enough to be a grave,' said Bob.

'Better get a CSI team up here,' said Sgt Moss. 'Looks like our boys may have had a falling out.'

'Or Maitland used that rope,' said Bob.

'Guess we'd better tell Pat,' said Sgt Moss. 'Hope he won't be too disappointed.'

When they returned to the shearing shed, Pat was watching the ambulance slowly make its way across the creek bed to start it's journey to Adelaide.

'Get anything out of him?' said Bob.

Pat shook his head. 'He's out of it. I'll have to wait until he comes out of surgery.'

'Is he going to make it?' said Sgt Moss.

'Paramedic reckons he'll survive,' said Pat. 'What did you boys find back there?'

'Looks like a grave,' said Bob.

'Probably Maitland,' said Sgt Moss, 'but we won't know for sure until you get CSI up here.'

Pat looked at Bob. He'd already discovered there was no signal on his mobile.

'I'll get on the blower,' said Bob, walking towards his vehicle.

While Bob used the radio in the Toyota to request a CSI team and arrange for additional resources to secure the scene until they arrived, the STAR Group officers returned in pairs from their sweep of the area and reported to Sgt Moss that the location was clear.

Sgt Moss stood his operatives down and directed them to prepare their vehicles for departure.

As the STAR Group officers were stowing their equipment, Bob rejoined Pat and Sgt Moss.

'All yours, gentlemen' said Sgt Moss. 'I'm done here.'

Bob looked at Pat, who didn't seem at all surprised by Sgt Moss' announcement. 'You staying or hitching a ride back with them?'

'I'll stay,' said Pat. 'Been a while since I've been camping.'

They leant on the front of the Toyota and watched the STAR Group operatives climb into their vehicles and leave in a cloud of dust.

'Weren't tempted to go with them?' said Bob.

'I've spent more than enough time with them,' said Pat. 'Too much bloody testosterone for my liking.'

Bob laughed. 'Got to admit that was a nice shot, though. If it had been me, Grant would be dead.'

'That might have something to do with them having automatic rifles with laser sights,' said Pat.

'Yeah,' said Bob. 'Bit easier than trying not to kill someone with a handgun.'

'Made a mess of his shoulder, though,' said Pat.

'We're going to need to rug up,' said Bob. 'Gets cold out here at night. Come on, I've got a couple of coats in the car.'

'Perhaps we can find somewhere to make a fire,' said Pat.

'We'll need to find somewhere inside one of these sheds to do that, I'm afraid. It's still fire danger season up here, which means no fires in the open.'

'Perhaps we could be civilised,' said Pat, 'and use the house. There's probably a wood burning stove in there somewhere.'

CHAPTER 30

By NOON ON TUESDAY, the body in the grave at Waterdown Station had been exhumed and identified as Paul Maitland. The pathologist gave the probable cause of death as asphyxiation due to hanging, subject to a full post mortem examination.

It was fairly obvious to Pat that John Grant had buried Paul's body, since he was the only other person at Waterdown Station at the time. The question Pat needed an answer to was whether Paul had hung himself or been killed with a rope.

He would have to wait until John Grant was deemed well enough to be interviewed, following surgery to his shoulder, to ask his questions. But at least he'd survived, and it looked like he'd live to face trial.

Pat packed his bag and went to find Lina. He was looking forward to going home and catching up with his daughter, and then spending a weekend in Darwin with his son now that the borders had reopened to vaccinated travellers.

On Wednesday morning, the doctor treating John Grant decided he was fit enough to be interviewed by police. It was two in the afternoon, though, by the time his lawyer arrived from Clare.

Pat didn't like bedside interviews. They had to rely on portable recording equipment and keep the proceedings short. If he was honest with himself, Pat didn't like hospitals. They reminded him of his loss and he started feeling uncomfortable as soon as they entered the ward where Grant was being held.

John Grant lay in his hospital bed, propped up with several pillows and attached to a machine displaying readings of his vital functions. There was an intravenous drip feeding a clear fluid into a vein in his right arm. His face looked gaunt, despite a suntan from years of exposure to the weather.

Under different circumstances, Pat would have felt sorry for him, but not today. Instead, he stood just inside the room, next to Grant's lawyer, loathing the man and waiting for Lina to set up their recording equipment, before stepping them through the required introductory remarks to start the interview.

'John Grant, I'm arresting you on suspicion of the murder of George Young,' said Pat, handing him a copy of the charges, 'and the murders of Jane Edwards and Andrew White, and advising you that anything you say may be recorded and used in evidence against you. Do you understand?'

'Yes,' said John, taking the sheet and handing it to his lawyer without looking at it.

'We'll be interviewing you later in relation to these charges,' said Pat. 'Today, I'd like to ask you a few questions about the death of Paul Maitland. Think you can handle that?'

John looked at his lawyer.

'You don't have to answer any of his questions, John.'

'He hung himself Sunday night while I was asleep,' said John.

'You bury him?' said Pat.

'Couldn't very well leave him where he was,' said John.

'Any idea why he hung himself?'

'I'd only be guessing,' said John. 'There are many reasons why a farmer commits suicide.'

'Want to tell me why you and Paul were at Waterdown Station?'

'No comment,' said John.

'Want to tell me why you didn't report the rifle your son found in your shed as missing?'

'No comment,' said John.

'That will do for today,' said Pat, realising there was no point asking questions if Grant was going to stonewall him with a series of no comment answers. 'Magistrate's hearing is set down for here at two, tomorrow afternoon. We'll be opposing bail.'

'I won't be going anywhere,' said John.

The only place you're going is prison, thought Pat, as he signalled to Lina that it was time to shut down the recording equipment.

Pat felt a sense of relief as they exited the hospital and walked to their car.

'How do you think he'll plead?' said Lina.

'He's guilty no matter how he pleads,' said Pat. 'He made a mistake, and he knows it.'

'The rifle?' said Lina.

They reached the car and got in. 'It was just as well we hadn't said anything about that cartridge found in the grave at Red Banks until after we'd matched it with the rifle,' said Pat. 'If he'd known about that he wouldn't have used that rifle to fake Young's suicide.'

Lina started the engine. 'That was another mistake in my book. Don't know why they didn't just dump the body with a plastic bag over its head.'

'Guess they didn't do enough research on the pathology of suffocation,' said Pat. 'Perhaps they hadn't watched enough crime shows on TV to realise we'd do a post mortem.'

'Yeah, right,' said Lina. 'I wonder why they killed him?'

'Something must have happened,' said Pat. 'Maybe he wanted to confess before he died. People do strange things when they know their days are numbered.'

Lina glanced at Pat before directing their car into the flow of traffic heading along North Terrace towards King William Street. 'You talking from experience there, Pat?'

'You know, my wife didn't talk to her mother for years. They had a falling out over something trivial. Something her mother accused her of doing behind her back, which Pam insisted she hadn't done. But her mother wouldn't believe her. Then her mother got breast cancer.'

'Didn't your wife die of breast cancer?'

'Runs in families, apparently. Anyway, her mother went downhill pretty fast. We only found out when Pam's sister called to let us know her mother wanted to apologise for not believing her.' Pat looked at Lina. 'She died three days after they reconciled.'

'How did you wife take that?'

'She cried for a week and then told me she'd been diagnosed with breast cancer, ' said Pat. 'She was dead eighteen months later.'

'Shit, that must have been hard.'

'It hasn't been easy but working with you has made a difference.' Pat smiled, hoping he hadn't upset her with his confession.

'Oh?' said Lina. 'In what way?'

'Let's just say you're a breath of fresh air after some of the other partners I've had, and I needed something like that. I'd sort of lost my way a bit. Started feeling sorry for myself.'

'You've got plenty of good years left in you, Pat.'

'They might not be in the job, though. I'm thinking of taking early retirement and trying my hand at something else.'

'I'll be sorry to see you go,' said Lina.

'It might not be for a while,' said Pat. 'I've got a few things to check out before I take the leap.'

CHAPTER 31

Rebecca sat in St Mary's, listening but not hearing, as Father Aiden delivered his sermon during the funeral service for Paul Maitland. Simon and Jarvis sat beside her, solemn expressions on their young faces. John's parents, sitting with heads bowed and hands in their laps, were on the other side of the boys. Her own parents sat next to her in the pew.

Three rows in front of them, Lorna Maitland sat with her sons, two boys of a similar age to her own who no longer had a father. Beside Lorna, Paul's parents sat like statues in dark clothes. The whole scene appeared a little surreal to Rebecca, as she took in the sight of the congregation of silent mourners in the soft glow of light the church's stained glass windows allowed into the building.

She glanced at the coffin. Although John was still alive, she thought he may as well be dead like Paul. His sons weren't going to be seeing much of him for the next twenty years, if at all. She certainly had no intention of visiting him in prison. It was hard enough being in the same room as Jarvis without seeing or thinking of John. At least Simon resembled the men on her side of the family.

She hoped John would change his plea to guilty and spare them the pain and embarrassment of a protracted trial. She couldn't believe he'd had the audacity to plead not guilty, given what she knew about the rifle and how its very existence exploded his alibi for the night Jane and Andrew had been murdered. The shame of being married to him for thirty years, after what he'd done, was more than she thought she could bear. She wanted it to end. She wanted the story to go away so they could get on with their lives. She did not want weeks of lurid reporting reminding her of the monster she had loved and shared her life with.

Father Aiden was talking about love and forgiveness. Rebecca dismissed those ideas as some ivory tower ideals. Her love had been betrayed. She'd trusted John. Given herself to him. But he'd lied to her. He'd lied to her about who he was and what he'd done. He'd lied to her about his relationship with Paul and said nothing about George. She wondered how many other secrets he had and then told herself she didn't want to know.

John had poisoned the lives of his sons before they'd been born, and then shattered their dreams through his thoughtless actions. There was no way in hell she'd be forgiving him, no matter what Jesus or anyone else had to say about the matter.

The service dragged on. Rebecca looked about her, surprised at the number of people who had decided to attend, given the circumstances. Then she reminded herself that being there was more about supporting the living than honouring the dead. She doubted if any of those present either understood or supported Paul's decision to end his life the way he had, but she knew everyone there felt for the family, felt for the wife and children he'd left behind.

She wondered what everyone thought and felt when it came to her and her children. Her husband and the father of her boys was still around to hate, and was in denial of his own guilt. She was sure he'd done it. What other reason was there to explain why he had run and fired at the police? And, if they were innocent, why had Paul ended his life the way he had? There was no other answer that she could see.

People were standing. Rebecca came out of her reverie. The service in the church was drawing to a close. The pall-bearers were assembling alongside the coffin, readying to accompany it on its journey down the aisle to the hearse waiting outside in the sunshine.

Following the interment at Burra Cemetery, the mourners gathered in St Mary's Church Hall for afternoon tea and a moment of social interchange. In a small place like Burra, a funeral was as much a social gathering as a celebration of the life of the deceased. People felt a genuine sorry for the family but they also enjoyed catching up with friends and neighbours they hadn't seen for a while.

It wasn't long before the hall was a buzz of sound, as people expressed their condolences and moved on to other topics of conversation.

After half an hour, the crowd began to thin as people departed to get on with their lives and Rebecca found herself sitting in a corner of the room with Lorna. They'd been friends for twenty five years. They'd married two men who had been friends since they'd started school. They'd compared notes on raising boys and being farmers' wives. Where Lorna had had the advantage of being a farmer's daughter and knowing how things worked on the land, Rebecca had been the one with the knowledge of how things worked in the wider world. Now, Rebecca felt as if they were both lost, neither having planned for the circumstances they faced.

'Good turnout,' said Rebecca.

'Glad it's bloody over,' said Lorna. 'At least now we'll be able to get on with our lives.'

'What have you decided?' said Rebecca. 'Are you staying?'

Lorna gazed past Rebecca to where their sons stood together at the end of a table, eating sausage rolls smothered in tomato sauce and chatting as if they were at the football. 'I think that will be best for the boys, don't you?'

Rebecca had had the same conversation with John's parents. What was in the best interest of the boys was simply a euphemism for what was in the best interests of the farm. When she'd asked her sons about what they should do, Jarvis had volunteered to switch to part-time study online so he could come home and run the farm with a little help from his grandfather and younger brother. Simon had simply shrugged. He'd always said he wanted to work on the farm with his brother.

'Do the boys want to stay on the farm?'

'David does,' said Lorna, 'but Sam's not sure what he wants to do yet.'

That made sense to Rebecca. Sam was a couple of years younger than Simon, too young to really know what he wanted to do with his life. 'Are they going back to school in Adelaide?'

'David wants to go back. It's his last year. But I'm not sure about Sam,' said Lorna, 'he only started boarding this year. He wants to come home and go to the Community School with his friends.'

'That could be good for you,' said Rebecca. 'Be better than being on your own.'

'I didn't want them to go in the first case,' said Lorna, 'but I lost that argument. Paul wasn't a fan of the local school.'

'That might have had something to do with what we know now,' said Rebecca.

Lorna crossed her arms. 'What's John going to do, Becky? Is he going to blame Paul?'

'I'm not sure. I don't understand why he didn't plead guilty.'

'You think they did it?'

Rebecca nodded. 'Why else did they take off after Simon asked John about the rifle he'd seen in the shed? John promised he'd report it missing to Bob Davenport, but he didn't.'

'And the police are sure that rifle was used to murder your friend?'

'Yes. They found a cartridge in the grave and John's father has confirmed the rifle was his.'

Lorna reached out and took Rebecca's hands. 'At least I have some sort of closure. Paul's not coming back whether he was involved in those murders or not. But you must be going through hell.'

'Hard to believe I've been married to the man who killed my best friends for twenty five years,' said Rebecca. 'I'm not sure I want to see him again, ever.'

'Not even if he's acquitted?' said Lorna.

'If he gets off it will be because of some smart lawyer.'

'What will you do then?'

'Honestly, I don't know. I hope he changes his mind and confesses.'

'But, what if they really are innocent?'

Rebecca looked Lorna in the eye. 'Then why did Paul hang himself, Lorna? Do you know of any other reason why he would do that?'

Lorna shook her head.

'No, the reason they ran, Lorna, was because they couldn't face the shame of people knowing what they'd done. They've left that for us to live with. I don't know about you, but I can't forgive them for that.'

'What are we going to do?' said Lorna.

'Stick together,' said Rebecca. 'We didn't do anything wrong and our boys are going to need us.'

Lorna smiled. 'I don't know how the olds are going to cope.'

'They'll find a way,' said Rebecca. 'We need to look out for ourselves.'

CHAPTER 32

LIFE inside the Remand Centre was nothing like John had imagined or experienced. The noise was unbearable. The sounds were harsh. Men called out. Doors clanged. Bells rang. The lights never went out. The guards dictated his daily routine.

John felt like a caged animal and yearned for the space and familiar silence of the farm, the silence of the great outdoors which was only broken by the sounds of nature. The only way he could find that silence and sense of spaciousness in his cell was to block out his surroundings and withdraw into himself.

And, it wasn't only the noise. There was also the fear, a dread he hadn't anticipated. He'd never been locked up with criminals before, men who were more familiar with the criminal justice system and knew how to intimidate others. John had always thought of himself as someone who could look after himself, but not in here.

They'd stripped him of his dignity during the admission process, reducing him to a shivering naked man with no defences. He'd never felt so humiliated.

When he mixed with the other inmates for meals and exercise, he felt exposed. He had no idea what was expected of him or who he could trust. He was as afraid of the guards as he was of his fellow inmates. Everyone was cold and indifferent.

After the first few days, he realised no-one really wanted to know him or have anything to do with him and began to relax. Everybody was too engrossed in their own circum-stances, wondering whether they'd beat the wrap or end up with a sentence they'd have to endure, to worry about him.

By the end of his first week, John had settled into the routine dictated by the Remand Centre's timetable and started looking forward to spending nights in the isolation of his cell.

John sat across the table from his lawyer. A guard sat on a chair outside the interview room.

'They've set a date in June,' said the lawyer.

'June?' said John. 'Do I have to stay in here until then? Can't they do it any sooner?'

'Courts are busy,' said the lawyer. 'The police haven't requested additional time to prepare their case.'

'That confident, are they?'

The lawyer smiled. 'I'm not sure they have much of a case. It all looks circumstantial to me.'

'What do you mean?' said John.

'They have a connection between the rifle found next to George Young and a cartridge found during an excavation in Red Banks. Who knows when that cartridge was fired, or if it's even connected to the bullet that killed Jane Edwards?

That's a hole big enough for us to sow some reasonable doubt.'

'Are you saying all I need is a story about shooting rabbits around where that cartridge was found to blow their case out of the water?'

The lawyer raised an eyebrow. 'Did you ever go hunting there with your father's twenty-two?'

John leant back in his chair and crossed his arms. He'd never been to Red Banks before that night or since. It would be so easy to lie but he realised he'd need a witness before anyone would believe him. 'No. I only ever used that rifle at our place.'

'What about your father?'

'You'd have to ask him,' said John, 'but I doubt it.'

The lawyer made a note on his pad. 'Did you hide that rifle in a shed on your farm?'

'Yeah,' said John.

'When?'

'Before I went back to school in 1992.'

'Why?'

'I didn't want to use it anymore,' said John. 'My father had given it to me. It had been a gift to him from his father. We had a fight after I failed and didn't get into Roseworthy. I hid it out of spite.'

'The police are saying your sons discovered the rifle sometime in 2020 but didn't say anything to you about it. Is that true?'

'I suppose,' said John. 'I hadn't moved it since I hid it.'

'And, the rifle was no longer where you'd hidden it when they told you about it?'

'It was gone.'

'How do you suppose that happened?' said the lawyer. 'That's one question the prosecutor is bound to ask.'

John shrugged. 'Anyone could have taken it. That shed's not locked. The boys could have told one of their friends about it. I don't know.'

'Do you have a dog on that farm of yours? Does it bark?'

'That wouldn't make much difference if we weren't home at the time.'

'Anything else missing from your shed?

'Not that I'm aware of,' said John.

'Did you report the theft?'

John looked down at his hands and slowly shook his head. He could see where this line of questioning was going and was certain he'd have to answer it in court in front of Rebecca and the boys. He wasn't sure he could do that and convince anyone he was telling the truth, since instead of reporting the theft he'd taken to the hills with Paul.

'According to the police, you told your wife you had reported it to the local sergeant, but you didn't, did you? How will you explain that in court?'

'I might have to tell the truth,' said John.

The lawyer leant forward. 'What did you say?'

'I'll have to tell the truth.'

The lawyer leant back and crossed his arms. 'And, what is the truth?'

'I took that rifle with me the day we went to have lunch with George,' said John, 'and left it with his body after we'd killed him.'

'Why did you kill George?'

John leant forward and rested his arms on the table. 'To keep him quiet. You see, George was there when Jane and

Andrew were killed, and he wanted money we didn't have in exchange for not breaking his silence.'

The lawyer stood. 'Sounds like you need to change your plea.'

John nodded. 'What happens now?'

'I'll need to have a chat with the DPP to see if we can get any concessions for a guilty plea.'

John lay on his bunk, staring at the ceiling and wondering if he'd live long enough to be released. His lawyer had told him to expect a life sentence of twenty five years, with a non-parole period of twenty. He'd be sixty eight by the time he might qualify for parole. Who'd want him in their life then? He was pretty sure Rebecca wouldn't be waiting around for him to be released. She wouldn't even come to see him while he was waiting to be sentenced.

He'd admitted his involvement in three murders but hadn't said anything about what they'd done to Jane before they'd killed her. That was a memory too painful to share. He'd take the details and the shame of his base behaviour on that night to the grave with him.

He'd spent the last thirty years regretting what he'd done that night. The whole thing had gotten out of hand because they'd misread Andrew, who'd had more raw courage than all three of them put together. He wasn't going to admit to Rebecca that he and his mates had raped her best friend before they'd shot her. He'd loved her and done his best by her as a husband. He'd never strayed, despite all the temptations. She was the best thing that had ever happened to him and she certainly didn't deserve what he'd done to her. What must she think of him now? He'd lied to her.

He wondered what his sons thought of him. He thought he'd been a good father. He'd learnt from his father's mistakes but, despite his good intentions, he'd disappointed them, since no son wanted to find out his father was a murderer who had killed someone before he was born.

He'd enjoyed being a father and teaching his boys the ways of living on the land. He knew Jarvis, who he'd schooled in regenerative agriculture and the responsibilities of sustainable farming, would take good care of the farm. He wasn't sure what Simon would do. He was too much like his mother.

John rolled over and looked at the wall. He told himself he should have gotten rid of the rifle, that he shouldn't have used it to make it look like George had committed suicide. If only he'd known about that bloody cartridge. If only they hadn't inadvertently buried it with the bodies. If only George had kept his word. If only they hadn't done it.

John turned to lie on his back again and put his hands behind his head. Maybe Paul had made the right decision. At least he wasn't living with the shame and the guilt. He'd left all that behind for his family to deal with.

He looked around his cell and wondered how that bloke in America he'd heard about on the news had managed to kill himself in his prison cell. He couldn't see a way to use anything in his cell to end his life, but wished he could.

He'd tried to get the police to shoot him when they'd turned up at Waterdown Station but they'd been too bloody professional. He rubbed his shoulder where the bullet had passed through him. It still hurt.

He looked up at the ceiling. There must be a reason why

he was still alive but he couldn't work out what it was, unless it was God's way of punishing him for what he'd done.

He closed his eyes and tried to imagine what the next twenty years would be like. As he thought about the years he'd spend inside, he was overcome by a sense of great unhappiness and loneliness. He opened his eyes into the glare of his cell and wished he was dead.

CHAPTER 33

Ross Sloane sat in his study with a glass of whiskey and an open file on the desk in front of him. The file was the private case file he'd opened thirty years ago, when the detectives had given up and put the disappearance of Jane Edwards and Andrew White into their too hard basket. The whiskey was from the bottle of Bushmills Black Bush that Mary had bought him for Christmas.

He'd had his suspicions about John Grant, Paul Maitland, and George Young right from the start but hadn't been able to break the story they'd concocted and stood by for thirty years.

He'd followed the recent case through the media after Bob Davenport had told him about the skeletal remains of Edwards and White being found buried in Red Banks Conservation Park. That was one place he hadn't searched. At the time, he'd considered the park, a playground for off-road recreational vehicle drivers, to be too far out of town and not the sort of place someone would hide a body. Ross sighed. He had to admit he'd been wrong on that score, even if his chances of finding a bush grave within the thousand hectares of the park would have been remote.

Was the choice of location a stroke of genius or sheer luck? He guessed he'd never know. Grant wasn't talking and the others were dead. Maybe it had something to do with George Young not living all that far from the park. Nothing he could do about it now, though. He'd just have to be satisfied they'd received sufficient climate-change inspired rain to wash away enough red soil to expose the contents of the grave.

John Grant had admitted shooting Jane Edwards and being present when Andrew White had been killed but he was refusing to give any details beyond what the police had established or to explain why they'd done it.

Ross leafed through his notes and stopped at the record of an interview he'd had with Sally Nelson in 1995. She'd told him the boys, especially John, had been a nuisance all through their years of high school, pestering her and her friends for sex. That was one of the reasons she'd given him for starting the book club and inviting Andrew to join them.

Ross wondered whether the whole thing was about the boys forcing Andrew to watch them have sex with Jane and things not going to plan. Andrew had been known as a nerd, someone who didn't know one end of a football from the other. Someone the other boys had bullied until the school had stepped in and talked to their parents.

Ross sat back and sipped his whiskey. It was starting to make sense. Grant was obviously too ashamed to admit what they'd done to his wife's best friend before they'd killed her.

He wondered what had triggered the fallout between the three friends after thirty years. They must have felt safe after Pat Travers' investigation had come up with nothing to indicate they had been involved. They'd even told Travers the same story they'd told him. But, obviously something had gone wrong and then it had all unravelled. Grant had made a mistake, several if he thought about it.

He wondered how young Simon felt about triggering his father's downfall by telling his mother about the rifle he'd found hidden in their shed. Poor lad. He must be devastated.

Ross wanted to ring that arrogant prick, Hamilton, the detective from Port Pirie who'd told him to butt out and leave it to the professionals, and rub it in but the prick was dead. And, what good would it have done even if he'd still been around?

Ross closed his file and put it back in his filing cabinet. At least now he could let it go. Justice had finally been served, even if it had taken thirty years.

CHAPTER 34

Sue Marshall sucked absent-mindedly on an arm of her glasses as she sat at her kitchen table and thought about what she wanted to say in her victim impact statement. She'd been denied thirty years of Jane's life and the opportunity of being a grandmother to her daughter's children, but the pain of her loss had long since gone.

Life had continued in the years following Jane's disappearance. She'd married and buried Kevin and become the grandmother of her stepson's daughter. She'd been in shock the day Bob Davenport had told her they'd found Jane and Andrew's remains, even though it had been news she'd been expecting for thirty years. She'd known all along Jane and Andrew were not coming home.

In a way, she and Cynthia had helped each other come to terms with what life had thrown at them. She had no way of knowing if Jane and Andrew would have stayed together if they'd lived but she and Cynthia had. They'd worked together, grieved together, and got on with life together.

It had been a greater shock learning they had been killed by John Grant and his friends. John's wife, Rebecca, had been Jane's best friend all through their school days and had always been there for her. She was like a daughter, and Sue had enjoyed watching her boys grow up.

She'd have to say something about that, about having to live with the knowledge of what John had done to Rebecca and her boys. And about the times he'd sat in her kitchen, sharing stories over a meal when Kevin had still been alive. Sue shuddered. The place suddenly felt dirty. Maybe it was time to sell up and move into the retirement village.

She got up, made herself a cup of tea and went out with it into the yard. Outside the air felt clean. She looked at her vegetable garden and watered the herbs next to the tank stand. She wasn't ready to walk away from her garden just yet. After all, she was only seventy. Young enough to have another man in her life if she was silly enough or lonely enough to go down that pathway. She laughed at the thought. There was no way that would be happening again. Two dead husbands were more than enough for any woman to deal with. She didn't want to go through that again.

She went back inside to call Cynthia to see what she and Michael were thinking about putting in their victim impact statement.

'Oh, we're thinking about not doing one,' said Cynthia.

'Why's that?' said Sue, her interest piqued.

'Michael reckons we've spent enough time feeling sorry for ourselves. Time to move on is what he says.'

Sue was a little mystified. The woman from the prosecutor's office had given her the impression the judge wanted to hear their statements before passing sentence. 'Don't you want the judge to take your feelings into account?'

'It's only an invitation to make a statement, Sue. You don't have to, you know,' said Cynthia. 'I'm sure the judge doesn't need to hear a sob story from us to work out the sentence he deserves.'

'I suppose you're right,' said Sue. 'It's not going to make any difference to me how long he spends in prison.'

There was a moment's silence and Sue wondered if she'd said something wrong.

'I don't know about you,' said Cynthia, 'I just don't want to think about it any more. We know what happened. We've given them a proper burial. I want to focus on the good things and enjoy the years we've got left.'

That made perfect sense to Sue. 'I'm glad we had this conversation, Cynthia. I was starting to feel guilty about feeling sorry for myself instead of reaching out to support Becky.'

'We should catch up with her,' said Cynthia, 'and let her know we're thinking about her.'

'Yeah, let's do that,' said Sue. 'I'll give her a call to arrange a get together and let you know.'

A NOTE FROM PETER

If you enjoyed **Desolation,** you can help other readers share your enjoyment by telling them about the book and writing a review.

Drop by at **www.petermulraney.com** and join my **Crime Readers Group** to download a free copy of **Deadly Sands,** and be one of the first to know when my next book will be released.

ALSO BY PETER MULRANEY

Inspector West series

After

The Holiday

Holy Death

Whistleblower

Twisted Justice

The East Park Syndicate

Inspector West Collection One

Inspector West Collection Two

Stella Bruno Investigates series

The Identity Thief

A Gun of Many Parts

Bones in the Forest

A Deadly Game of Hangman

Taken

Fallout

The Melrose Case

The Scam

Deception

Stella Bruno Investigates: Books 1 to 6

The Identity Thief Collection

The Fallout Collection

The Deception Collection

Ryan Holiday PI Short Stories

Rosie

Framed

Novella

The New Girlfriend

Living Alone series

After She's Gone

Cooking 4 One

Sanity Savers

Living Alone (Collection)

Living Alone Journal

Everyday Business Skills

Everyday Project Management

Everyday Productivity

Everyday Money Management

Writings of the Mystic

Sharing the Journey: Reflections of a Reluctant Mystic

My Life is My Responsibility: Insights for Conscious Living

I Am Affirmations: The Power of Words

Beyond the Words: Reflections on I Am Affirmations

Mystical Journey: A Handbook for Modern Mystics

Sharing the Journey Coloring Books

Mandalas

Mandalas by 3

Sharing the Journey Coloring Journals

Sharing the Journey Coloring Journal

Sharing the Journey Coloring Journal ~Discovery

Sharing the Journey Coloring Journal ~ Reflection

www.ingramcontent.com/pod-product-compliance
Lightning Source LLC
Chambersburg PA
CBHW020514120726
47904CB00003B/821